Ben Jonson's Sejanus' Fall: A Retelling

David Bruce

Published by David Bruce, 2022.

BEN JONSON'S SEJANUS' FALL: A RETELLING

First edition. July 10, 2022.

Copyright © 2022 David Bruce.

ISBN: 979-8201448189

Written by David Bruce.

Table of Contents

The cover shows a man who is more unscrupulous than Sejanus. Vladimir Putin is a killer of Ukrainian pregnant women and of Ukrainian children and is damn proud of it. My association of him with a fall is, unfortunately, probably wishful thinking.

The Roman Republic was a time of freedom for many, but when the Roman Empire started, the Emperor gained the power that others lost. Briefly, Russia had some freedom: Gorbachev promoted social democracy. Putin stopped a democracy from forming, and with the war against Ukraine, he stopped free speech.

Tiberius served his country poorly as Emperor. The United States has had a recent President who served the United States poorly.

Buy a bottle of booze now and set it aside because when certain politicians die, the booze stores will run out of product.

Dedicated to Carl Eugene Bruce and Josephine Saturday Bruce

***

Educate Yourself

Read Like A Wolf Eats

Be Excellent to Each Other

Books Then, Books Now, Books Forever

***

In this retelling, as in all my retellings, I have tried to make the work of literature accessible to modern readers who may lack some of the knowledge about mythology, religion, and history that the literary work's contemporary audience had.

Do you know a language other than English? If you do, I give you permission to translate this book, copyright your translation, publish or self-publish it, and keep all the royalties for yourself. (Do give me credit, of course, for the original retelling.)

I would like to see my retellings of classic literature used in schools, so I give permission to the country of Finland (and all other countries) to buy one copy of this eBook and give copies to all students forever. I also give permission to the state of Texas (and all other states) to buy one copy of this eBook and give copies to all students forever. I also give permission to all teachers to buy one copy of this eBook and give copies to all students forever.

Teachers need not actually teach my retellings. Teachers are welcome to give students copies of my eBooks as background material. For example, if they are teaching Homer's *Iliad* and *Odyssey*, teachers are welcome to give students copies of my *Virgil's* Aeneid: *A Retelling in Prose* and tell students, "Here's another ancient epic you may want to read in your spare time."

THE ARGUMENT
[Summary of Subject Matter]

Sejanus' Early History and Disgrace by Drusus Senior

Aelius Sejanus was the son of Seius Strabo, a gentleman of Rome, and he was born at Vulsinium.

After his long service in court, first under Augustus, and afterward under Tiberius, Sejanus grew into such favor with Tiberius, and won him by his arts, that there lacked nothing but the name to make him a co-partner of the Empire.

Drusus Senior, the Emperor's son, did not like and did not tolerate this greatness of Sejanus. After many smothered dislikes, his dislike one day broke out, and Drusus Senior struck Sejanus publicly on the face.

To revenge this disgrace and to learn Drusus Senior's plans and secrets, Sejanus conspired and plotted with Livia, the wife of Drusus Senior. Livia was seduced by Sejanus to her dishonor before the plot to kill Drusus Senior proceeded, Sejanus also plotted together with her physician, who was called Eudemus, and with a man called Lygdus, who was a eunuch, to poison Drusus Senior.

Sejanus Grows Ambitious to Become Emperor

Their inhuman act had successful and not-suspected passage — the death of Drusus Senior aroused no suspicion — and it emboldened Sejanus to farther and more insolent projects, leading even to his ambition of becoming Emperor.

Finding the obstacles and hindrances he must encounter to be many and hard, in respect of the descendants of Germanicus (who were next in line for the succession), Sejanus devised to make Tiberius' self his means, and instilled into his ears many doubts and suspicions both against the princes and against their mother, Agrippina.

Tiberius jealously hearkening to these things, he as ardently as Sejanus consented to their ruin and to their friends' ruin.

Sejanus Plots to Marry Livia and Plots Against Tiberius

In this time, the better to mature and strengthen his design, Sejanus labored to marry Livia, and worked with all his ingenuity and cunning to remove

Tiberius from the knowledge of public business, with allurements of a quiet and retired life, the latter of which Tiberius (out of a proneness to lust and a desire to hide those unnatural pleasures that he could not so publicly practice) embraced.

Sejanus' Downfall

Sejanus' desire to marry Livia enkindled Tiberius' fears and gave him the first reason to fear and be suspicious of Sejanus. Against Sejanus, Tiberius raised in private a new instrument to do his bidding, one Sertorius Macro, and by use of Macro, Tiberius took clandestine measures and worked against Sejanus, discovered the other's plots and secrets, his means and his ends, and sounded the affections of the Senators, who were divided into factions, and distracted them.

At last, when Sejanus least looked for trouble and was most secure, Tiberius decoyed and enticed him away from his guards with the pretext of doing him an unwonted honor in the Senate; and with a long, ambiguous, and equivocal letter, in one day he had Sejanus suspected, accused, condemned, and torn into pieces by the rage of the people.

Ben Jonson Gives His Reason for Writing This Tragedy

This play we advance as a mark of terror to all traitors and treasons, to show how just the heavens are in pouring and thundering down a weighty vengeance on their unnatural intents, even to the worst princes; much more to those for guard of whose piety and virtue the angels are in continual watch, and God himself miraculously working.

CAST OF CHARACTERS

MALE CHARACTERS

Tiberius. Second Roman Emperor. Successor to Caesar Augustus, who was his step-father and adoptive father. Ruled from 14-37 C.E. He was the father of Drusus Senior and the uncle of Germanicus. At birth he was named Tiberius Claudius Nero. After becoming Emperor, he was known as Tiberius Caesar Augustus. Tiberius is often referred to as Caesar.

Drusus Senior. He was the son of Tiberius and his first wife: Vipsania. He was the second husband of Livia. First in line of succession to Tiberius.

Sejanus. He was Consul in the first half of 31 C.E. Sejanus' father was a knight, and so Sejanus was a member of the equestrian (knight) class of citizens, which were ranked just below the noble class. He was executed in 31 C.E.

Nero. He was the oldest son of Germanicus, who was Tiberius' nephew and adopted son, and Agrippina. Sejanus plotted against him. Second in line of succession to Tiberius. This Nero is NOT the Nero who became the fifth Roman Emperor. That Nero was born in 54 C.E., well after the events of Jonson's play, which ends in 31 C.E.

Latiaris. Supporter of Sejanus. Betrayer of Sabinus.

Drusus Junior. Second son to Germanicus and Agrippina. Third in line of succession to Tiberius. Drusus "Junior" means Drusus "the Younger." When Germanicus died, however, Drusus Senior took care of Drusus Junior.

Varro. Follower of Sejanus.

Caligula. Youngest son of Germanicus and Agrippina. Fourth in line of succession to Tiberius. "Caligula" is a nickname that means "Little Military-Boot." He succeeded Tiberius and became the third Roman Emperor.

Macro. *Vigiles* (Watch, Night Watch, Police, Firefighters) Prefect. Enemy to Sejanus. Sertorius Macro.

Arruntius. A Senator of good character. Lucius Arruntius.

Cotta. A man without scruples.

Silius. A general under Germanicus. Caius Silius.

Afer. An excellent orator with excessive ambition.

Sabinus. A knight. Close to Agrippina, the widow of Germanicus, who had been his friend. Titius Sabinus.

Haterius. An orator well noted for the style of his orations. Noted for the content of his orations? Not so much.

Lepidus. A Senator of integrity and capability. Marcus Lepidus.

Sanquinius. A Senator.

Cordus. An historian and defender of free speech. Cremutius Cordus.

Pomponius. A follower of Sejanus.

Gallus. Husband of Vipsania, who had been Tiberius' first wife.

Postumus. An underling of Sejanus. The name "Postumus" means "born after the death of the father." Julius Postumus.

Regulus. Opponent to Sejanus.

Trio. Consul on the side of Sejanus.

Terentius. Friend to Sejanus.

Minutius. Friend to Sejanus.

Laco. Commander of the *Vigiles* (Watch, Night Watch, Police, Firefighters). Gracinus Laco.

Satrius. Client of Sejanus. Satrius Secundus.

Eudemus. Physician to Livia.

Natta. Client of Sejanus. Pinnarius Natta.

Rufus. An ex-Praetor. Supporter of Sejanus. Enemy to Sabinus.

Opsius. Supporter of Sejanus. Enemy to Sabinus.

Tribuni. Military Tribunes of the Praetorian Guard.

FEMALE CHARACTERS

Agrippina. Widow of Germanicus. She was the granddaughter of Caesar Augustus. Her mother was Julia, Caesar Augustus' daughter. In history, she is known as Agrippina the Elder.

Livia. Lover of Sejanus. Husband to Drusus Senior. Sister to Germanicus. In history, she is known as Livilla, a nickname meaning "Little Livia." She was named after Livia Drusilla, the third and final wife of Caesar Augustus. She was the sister of Claudius, who became the fourth Roman Emperor.

Sosia. Wife of Silius. Friend of Agrippina.

MINOR CHARACTERS

Praecones. Heralds. Criers in meetings of the Senate. This book uses the word "Heralds."

Lictors. They held the *fasces* — a bundle of rods and an axe that served as a symbol of power — as they preceded magistrates through the streets.

Flamen. Priest. This book uses the word "Priest" rather than "Flamen."

Ministri. Attendants. This book uses the word "attendants."

Tubicines. Trumpeters. This book uses the word "trumpeters."

Tibicines. Flautists. This book uses the word "flautists."

Nuntius. Messenger. This book uses the word "messenger."

Servi. Servants. The singular is "servus." This book uses the word "servant."

Praetor. Second in rank to a Consul.

Guards.

The Scene: Rome

NOTES:

In this retelling, I use the scene divisions that appear in this book: Ben Jonson, *Sejanus his Fall*. W. F. Bolton, editor. A New Mermaid Dramabook. New York: Hill and Wang, 1966. I, however, did add a scene division — scene 4 — to Act 2, and a scene division — scene 3 — to Act 3 and a scene division — scene 5 — to Act 4. I also added two scene divisions to Act 5. In making scene divisions, I followed the practice of starting a new scene after everyone has exited.

Germanicus, having died in 19 C.E., does not appear in the play. He was the nephew and adopted son of Tiberius.

Tiberius, the second Roman Emperor, was born in 42 B.C.E. and died in 37 C.E. He ruled from 14 C.E. to 37 C.E. and was succeeded by Caligula.

Sejanus was born in 20 B.C.E. and died in 31 C.E.

Sejanus wanted to succeed Tiberius as Emperor, but some of Tiberius' relatives were in his way. These men were eligible to succeed Tiberius:

• Drusus Senior. The son of Tiberius and his first wife: Vipsania. First to be expected to succeed.

• Nero. First son to Germanicus and Agrippina. Nero was Tiberius' nephew and adopted son. Second to be expected to succeed.

• Drusus Junior. Second son to Germanicus and Agrippina. Third to be expected to succeed.

• Caligula. Third son to Germanicus and Agrippina. He would eventually succeed Tiberius.

In Ben Jonson's society, a person of higher rank would use "thou," "thee," "thine," and "thy" when referring to a person of lower rank. (These terms were also used affectionately and between equals.) A person of lower rank would use "you" and "your" when referring to a person of higher rank.

"Sirrah" was a title used to address someone of a social rank inferior to the speaker. Friends, however, could use it to refer to each other.

The word "wench" at this time was not necessarily negative. It was often used affectionately.

Roman Offices

Consuls: The office of Consul was the highest political office of the Roman Republic. Two Consuls were elected each year and served for one year.

Praetors: A Praetor can be 1) the commander of an army, or 2) a magistrate. The office of Praetor (magistrate) was the second highest political office of the Roman Republic. They were subject only to the veto of the Consuls. Praetors could take the auspices, the performance of which was a religious rite.

Lictors: Lictors served the Consuls and carried rods and axes as symbols of the Senators' authority. Rods were symbols of the Consuls' power to inflict corporal punishment, and axes were symbols of their power to inflict capital punishment. Lictors executed punishments on people who had been convicted of serious crimes.

Tribunes: Tribunes were administrative officers. Some were judicial Tribunes, and some were military Tribunes.

Aediles: An Aedile was a Roman magistrate who was in charge of maintaining public buildings. They also organized public festivals and were in charge of weights and measures.

Censors: They supervised public morality and maintained the census.

Prefects: They had civil or military power, but that power was delegated to them from others.

Praecones: Heralds. Criers in meetings of the Senate. They cry loudly things during a trial, such as "Silence!"

CHAPTER 1

— 1.1 —

Sabinus and Silius met each other.

Silius had been a general under Germanicus, the nephew and adopted son of Tiberius, who was currently the Roman Emperor, after having succeeded Caesar Augustus.

Sabinus, a knight, was close to Agrippina, the widow of Germanicus, who had been his friend.

"Hail, Caius Silius!" Sabinus greeted his friend.

"Titius Sabinus, hail!" Silius replied. "You're rarely — seldom and splendidly — met in court."

"Therefore, we are well met," Sabinus replied.

"It is true; indeed, this place — the court — is not our sphere," Silius said.

Neither man liked the court or the politics that occurred in the court.

Sabinus said:

"No, it isn't, Silius. We are no good at being plotters and schemers.

"We lack the 'fine' arts of conspiring and their thriving use that should make us graced or favored of the times.

"We have no successive changes of faces to use in duplicity, no cleft tongues, no soft and glutinous bodies that can stick like snails on painted walls, or on our breasts creep up like a snake, to fall from that proud height to which we did climb by slavery, not by service."

One way to climb to wealth and office is through slavery: being servile to those men who are in high office. When Caesar Augustus assumed power, the boldest men opposing him had died, and those who were willing to be subservient to him were rewarded.

Sabinus continued:

"We are no guilty men, and therefore we are no great men.

"We have no place in court, no office in state that we can say we have due to our crimes."

Another way to climb to wealth and office is through committing crimes, a word that can also mean sins.

Sabinus continued:

"We burn with no black secrets —"

Black secrets can make one susceptible to being servile to the man who knows one's black secrets. And if you are the one who knows black secrets, it can make other men — the ones with black secrets — servile to you.

One wonders what black secrets Vladimir Putin (killer of Ukrainian pregnant women and babies) knows about Donald Trump.

Sabinus continued:

"— black secrets that can make us dear to the pale authors —"

"Dear" can mean "costly." Paying blackmail to the man who knows one's black secrets can be costly. Buying someone's silence is expensive. The pale authors of the black secrets would pay much money and/or render other services to Silius and Sabinus — if Silius and Sabinus knew any black secrets.

In addition, the people paying the blackmail can treat the blackmailers well out of fear of arousing their anger — anger that could result in making black secrets known.

Sabinus and Silius neither had nor knew any black secrets.

Sabinus continued:

"— or make us live in fear of the still-waking anger of those being blackmailed, to raise ourselves a fortune by subverting and destroying theirs."

One way to raise and advance oneself is by causing someone else to fall.

Sabinus continued:

"We stand not in the lines that advance to that so courted point."

Lines of people seek a point — a goal — that points to the court.

Satrius and Natta entered the scene. Both men were clients of Sejanus, who was their patron. Sejanus supported them, and in return, the clients were bound to serve him and protect his life.

Silius said, "But yonder lean a pair who do."

The pair leaned toward the side of doing bad deeds to advance themselves. Satrius and Natta were not morally upright. They leaned on Sejanus for support. They supported Sejanus, and in turn he supported them. But clearly they knew that Sejanus was the alpha male.

Latiaris entered the scene. He supported Sejanus.

"Good cousin Latiaris," Sabinus greeted him.

In this society, the word "cousin" meant "kinsman."

Silius and Sabinus talked together at the side as Latiaris joined Satrius and Natta.

Silius said:

"Satrius Secundus and Pinnarius Natta, the great Sejanus' clients: There are two men who know more than honest counsels.

"Their close breasts and secret hearts, if they were ripped up and opened to light, would show that it would be a poor and idle sin to which their trunks had not been made fit organs."

In other words: Closely examine their hearts, and you will hardly find a sin that they have not committed.

Silius continued:

"These two men can lie, flatter, and swear, forswear [swear falsely], defame and disparage, inform on traitors or 'traitors,' smile, and betray; make men 'guilty,' and then beg the forfeit lives to get the livings."

People could grow wealthy by informing on traitors or "traitors." As a reward for their information, they would acquire some of the convicted man's property as a reward. These informers would "beg" to get wealth and property. The penalty for treason was usually a horrible death.

Silius continued:

"These two men can cut men's throats with whisperings; they can sell to gaping suitors the empty smoke — empty promises — that flies about the palace."

The Roman proverb *fumum vendere* means literally "to sell smoke" and figuratively "to make empty promises."

Silius continued:

"These two men can laugh when their patron laughs, sweat when he sweats, be hot and cold with him, and change every mood, demeanor, and garb, as often as he varies.

"These two men observe their patron as his watch observes his clock."

A soldier of the Night Watch could be observing the time, or a man could be checking the time on his watch against a public clock. In other words, Satrius and Natta observe Sejanus — their patron — closely and often.

Silius continued:

"And, true as turquoise in the dear lord's ring, these two men look well or ill, according to how their patron, Sejanus, looks."

Turquoise was believed to change color according to the health of its wearer.

Silius continued:

Satrius and Natta are ready to praise his Lordship — Sejanus — if he spits, or simply pisses fair, if he should have an indifferent stool, or if he breaks wind well.

"Nothing can escape their notice."

Sabinus said:

"Alas, these things deserve no note, compared with other vile and filthier flatteries that corrupt the times, when not alone the great personages of the state are eager to make their safety and security by doing such sordid acts, but all our Consuls, and no little part of such as have been Praetors — yea, the most of Senators, who otherwise do not use their voices, start up in public Senate, and there strive who shall propound the most abject, despicable, and base things, so much that often Tiberius has been heard, while leaving the court, to cry, 'O race of men, prepared for servitude!'

"This showed that he, who least the public liberty could like, as loathly brooked their abject servility."

To advance themselves, highly ranked bad men would flatter the Emperor Tiberius, who knew that they were flattering him and who loathed — or appeared to loath —such flattery and such bad men.

Silius said:

"Well, all is deserved by us — and we deserve more — who with our riots and debauches, pride, and civil hate have so provoked the justice of the gods.

"We who within these fourscore years were born free, equal lords of the conquered world, and knew no masters but passions, to which, betraying first our liberties, we since became the slaves to one man's lusts, and now to many."

Not too long ago, the Romans had enjoyed a republic. Julius Caesar had fought a civil war and seemed to be on the verge of becoming a King or an Emperor, but Brutus and Cassius had assassinated him. A new civil war had broken out, and Caesar Augustus had become the first Roman Emperor. When he died, Tiberius succeeded him.

Sabinus and Silius mourned the loss of the old Roman Republic. They believed that they had lost much freedom in the new Roman Empire.

Silius continued:

"Every ministering spy who will accuse and swear is lord of you, of me, of all, and of all our fortunes and our lives.

"Our looks are called into question, and our words, howsoever innocent, are made crimes.

"We shall shortly not dare to tell our dreams, or think, but it will be treason."

Greedy men would closely listen to other people's words, hoping that those other people would say something that could be twisted and interpreted as treasonous. Greedy men could turn in traitors and "traitors" and profit by so doing.

Sabinus said:

"Tyrants' arts are to give flatterers grace, accusers power,

"So that those [flatterers and accusers] may seem to kill whom they [tyrants] devour."

Cordus and Arruntius entered the scene.

Cordus was a historian and a defender of free speech, and Arruntius was a Senator of good character.

Sabinus said, "Now here is good Cremutius Cordus."

Cordus replied to Sabinus, "Hail to Your Lordship!"

Silius, Sabinus, Cordus, and Arruntius walked aside and whispered together.

Natta asked, "Who is that man who greets your cousin Sabinus?"

Latiaris answered, "He is named Cordus, a gentleman of Rome. He has written historical annals recently, they say, and very well."

"Annals?" Natta said. "Of what times?"

"I think of Pompey's, and Caius Julius Caesar's, and so down to these," Latiaris replied.

Pompey was a general whom Julius Caesar defeated in a civil war.

Natta asked, "How stands he inclined to the present state? Is he either Drusian, or Germanican? Or ours, or neutral?"

Tiberius' time was marked by factionalism. Political factions supported Drusus Senior, or Germanicus' relatives, or Sejanus.

"I don't know him well enough to know that," Latiaris replied.

"Those times are somewhat hazardous and unsettled to be touched," Natta said. "Have you either seen or heard part of his work?"

"No," Latiaris said. "He intends that they shall be public shortly."

"Oh," Natta said. "Do you call him Cordus?"

"Aye," Latiaris said.

Satrius, Natta, and Latiaris exited.

Sabinus said, "But these our times are not the same, Arruntius."

Arruntius replied:

"These our times?

"The men, the men are not the same; we are base, poor, and degenerated from the exalted strain of our great fathers.

"Where is now the soul of god-like Cato the Younger? — he who dared to be good when Julius Caesar dared to be evil; and who had the power not to live as Julius Caesar's slave, but instead to die as his master.

"Or where is now the loyal Brutus, who being proof against all the charm and allurement of benefits and favors did strike so brave a blow into the monster's heart that sought unnaturally to make captive and enslave his country?

"Oh, they have fled the light."

Cato the Younger had fought against Julius Caesar. When Cato's side was defeated, he committed suicide rather than live on in what he considered would be a tyranny under Julius Caesar.

Brutus and Cassius led the plot that led to the assassination of Julius Caesar.

Arruntius continued:

"Those mighty spirits lie raked up with their ashes in their urns, and not a spark of their eternal fire glows in a present bosom; all's but a momentary blaze of brightness, flashes, and smoke, wherewith we labor so, there's nothing Roman in us, nothing good, gallant, or great.

"What Cordus says is true: 'Brave Cassius was the last of all that race.'"

"Stand aside!" Sabinus said. "Lord Drusus is coming."

Drusus Senior and Haterius entered the scene.

"The Emperor's son!" Haterius shouted. "Give place! Make room!"

Arruntius, Silius, Cordus, and Sabinus stood to the side as Drusus Senior and Haterius walked around.

Drusus Senior was expected to succeed Tiberius, and Haterius was an orator.

"I like the prince well," Silius said.

Drusus Senior and Haterius exited.

"Drusus Senior is a riotous youth," Arruntius said. "There's little hope of him."

"His age will, as it grows, correct that fault of being riotous," Sabinus said. "I think he bears himself each day more nobly than the previous day; and he wins no less on men's affections than his father loses. Believe me, I love him, and I love him chiefly for his opposing Sejanus."

Silius said, "And I love him for gracing his young kinsmen so, the sons of Prince Germanicus; it shows a gallant clearness in him, a straight and upright mind that does not maliciously envy their father's name in them."

Drusus Senior, who opposed Sejanus, had a reputation for partying, but most Roman citizens forgave him that because of his youth and good deeds.

Drusus Senior had acted as a father to the sons of the deceased general Germanicus. Drusus Senior was the son of Tiberius, and Germanicus had been the adopted son of Tiberius, and so Drusus Senior and Germanicus had been step-brothers.

Germanicus' sons were Nero, Drusus Junior, and Caius, who was nicknamed Caligula and would eventually succeed Tiberius.

"The name of Germanicus was, while he lived, above and superior to all malicious envy; and now that he is dead, is without all malicious envy," Arruntius said. "Oh, that man! If there were seeds of the old moral virtue and valor left, they lived in him."

Silius said:

"He had the fruits, Arruntius, more than the seeds."

The fruits of virtue include justified fame and good reputation.

Dead or alive, Germanicus was respected.

Silius continued:

"Sabinus and I myself had the means and opportunity to know him inside and out, and we can report on him and his true character.

"We were his followers, but he would call us his friends.

"Germanicus was a man most like to virtue in all and every action.

"He was nearer to the gods than men in nature, of a body as fair as was his mind, and no less worthy of reverence in face than fame.

"He could so use his state and high rank, tempering his greatness with his gravity, so that it banished and sent away all self-love in him and spite in others.

"What his funerals lacked in images and pomp, they had supplied with honorable sorrow — soldiers' sadness — a kind of silent mourning, suitable for such men who know no tears except those that their captives are accustomed to show in very great losses."

The soldiers remained silent while mourning because they associated tears with their captives.

Cordus said, "I thought once, considering their outward forms and appearances, age, manner of deaths, the nearness of the places where they died, to have paralleled him with great Alexander, for both were of the best features and appearance, of high race and exalted heritage, aged but to thirty at their deaths, and in foreign lands, by their own people, alike made away."

Plutarch's *Lives* paired one Greek biography with one Roman biography.

Cordus had thought of pairing the biography of the Roman Germanicus with the biography of the Greek Alexander the Great. Both were remarkable men, and both were rumored to have died young after being poisoned.

Plutarch was born in 46 C.E. and so was not yet born at the time Ben Jonson's play was set. Plutarch did write about Alexander the Great, but he paired Alexander with Julius Caesar.

Sabinus disagreed that Germanicus should be compared to Alexander the Great, who was from Macedon and who died after a drinking bout:

"I don't know about Germanicus' death, how you might wrest and interpret it. But as for his life, it did as much disdain comparison with that voluptuous, rash, giddy, and drunken Macedonian's life as mine does with my bondman's — my slave's.

"All the good in Alexander — his valor and his fortune — Germanicus made his. But he had other touches of late Romans that more did describe and proclaim who Germanicus was.

"He had Pompey's dignity; the innocence, blamelessness, and uprightness of Cato; Caesar's spirit; wise Brutus' temperance.

"Every virtue that, imparted to others, gave them good name and good reputation, flowed mixed all together in him."

In other words: Virtues that went singly and individually to some great men, had all grouped together and had all gone to Germanicus.

Sabinus continued his praise of Germanicus:

"He was the soul of goodness, and all our praises of him are like streams drawn from a spring that still rise full and leave the part remaining greatest."

All their praises of Germanicus could not do justice to his goodness.

Arruntius said, "I am sure that he was too great for us, and that they knew who did remove him hence."

These words can mean 1) the people who poisoned Germanicus knew how good a man he was, and/or 2) important people knew who were the people who had poisoned Germanicus.

Tiberius was rumored, influenced by his mother, to have had Germanicus poisoned because of malicious envy of him. To do that, he had Germanicus serve far from Rome. Germanicus died in Antioch, which is near the modern city of Antakya in Turkey.

Sabinus said:

"When men grow securely and deeply honored and loved, there is a trick in state, which jealous princes never fail to use, how to deflect and thwart that growth with fair pretext and honorable appearances of employment, either by embassy, the war, or such, to shift them forth into another air, where they may purge, and lessen; so was Germanicus securely and deeply honored and loved, and he had his seconds — his secondaries — there, sent by Tiberius and his more subtle dam — his mother, Livia, the wife of Caesar Augustus — to discontent him, to breed and cherish mutinies, detract his greatest actions, give audacious check to his commands, and work to put him out in open act of treason."

Thee seconds were Gnaeus Calpurnius Piso and his wife Plancina, who were thought to have poisoned Germanicus and killed him. Piso was governor of Syria when Germanicus was reorganizing Rome's Asian provinces and kingdoms.

Sabinus continued:

"When his wise cares prevented all of these snares, a fine poison was thought on to mature their practices."

"Here comes Sejanus," Cordus said.

"Now observe the stoops, the bendings, and the falls," Silius said.

The followers of Sejanus were obsequious and frequently bended the knee and bowed to him. One or both knees would fall to the ground.

A fall can also be a moral decline or a trap to ensnare others.

"Most creeping base!" Arruntius said.

Sejanus' base, aka followers, were base.

Sejanus, Satrius, Terentius, and some other followers of Sejanus entered the scene.

Terentius was a friend to Sejanus, and Satrius was one of Sejanus' clients. Satrius pointed to the group of men who admired Germanicus and did not admire Sejanus: Arruntius, Cordus, Sabinus, and Silius.

Sejanus said to Satrius, "I note them well. No more. What do you have to say to me?"

Satrius began, "My lord, there is a gentleman of Rome who would buy —"

"What do you call the man whom you talked with?" Sejanus interrupted.

"Please Your Lordship, he is Eudemus, the physician to Livia, the wife of Drusus Senior," Satrius said.

Livia was Germanicus' sister and Tiberius' niece.

Sejanus said, "Continue on with your suit. He would buy, you said —"

"A Tribune's place, my lord," Satrius said.

Eudemus wanted to buy the political position of Tribune. He could do that by bribing Sejanus.

"What will he give?" Sejanus asked.

Satrius answered, "Fifty sestertia."

"Livia's physician, you say, is that fellow?" Sejanus asked.

"He is, my lord," Satrius said. "What is your Lordship's answer?"

"Answer to what?" Sejanus said.

"The place, my lord," Satrius said. "It is for a gentleman whom your Lordship will well like when you see him, and one you may make yours by the grant."

By making him a Tribune, Sejanus could make a follower of Eudemus, the physician to Livia, the wife of Drusus Senior.

"Well, let him bring his money and his name," Sejanus said.

The word "name" can mean "reputation."

Satrius said, "I thank Your Lordship. He shall, my lord."

"Come closer," Sejanus said.

He asked quietly, "Do you know this same Eudemus? Is he learned?"

Satrius answered, "He is reputed to be learned, my lord, and of deep practice."

"Deep practice" can mean 1) learned medical practice, and/or 2) treacherous practices.

Sejanus said quietly, "Bring him in to me, in the gallery [a long, narrow apartment], and find a reason to leave him and me there, together. I want to confer with him about an ailment."

He then said out loud, "Let's continue on our way."

Sejanus, Satrius, Terentius, and some other supporters and clients of Sejanus exited; a few other supporters and clients of Sejanus remained.

Arruntius said:

"So, yet another? Yet? Oh, desperate state of groveling honor!"

They had just witnessed a bribe.

Because such honors as Tribuneships could be purchased with groveling bribes, they were groveling honors.

Arruntius continued:

"See thou this, O sun, and do we see thee after?

"I think that day should lose its light when men do lose their shames and for the empty circumstance — trivial details — of life betray their cause of living, aka their reason for living."

Juvenal in his eighth Satire, wrote, in G.G. Ramsay's translation, "[...] count it the greatest of all sins to prefer life to honor, and to lose, for the sake of living, all that makes life worth having" (lines 83-84).

Freedom makes life worth having. Why give up your freedom to bribe your way into a political office? Bribing someone demonstrates that that person is your superior.

Eudemus was going to both give money to Sejanus and become beholden to him.

Silius said in reply to Arruntius:

"Not so."

Men do evil, and the day keeps its light. The natural world does not necessarily punish evil men. Indeed, Sejanus now appeared to have more power than the natural world.

Silius continued:

"Sejanus can repair, if Jove — Jupiter, the King of the gods — should ruin.

"Sejanus is the now — current — court-god; and well applied to and supplicated by the sacrifice of knees, of crooks, and cringe — the knees bend and kneel to him — he will do more than all the house of heaven can, for a thousand hecatombs."

Hecatombs of 100 oxen per hecatomb are public sacrifices to the gods. A thousand hecatombs would require the sacrifice of 100,000 oxen.

Silius continued:

"It is he who makes us our day, or night; hell and Elysium are in his look; we talk of the judge Rhadamanth in the Land of the Dead, the avenging spirits known as the Furies, and fire-brands — those already burning or destined to burn in hell — but it is his frown that is all these, where on the adverse part — the opposite side — his smile is more than poets ever yet feigned, aka invented, of bliss and cool, leafy shades, the gods' drink that is called nectar —"

Arruntius said about Sejanus:

"A serving boy!

"I knew him at Caius Caesar's table, when for hire he prostituted his abused body to that great gourmand, fat Apicius, and was the noted pathic — boy prostitute — of the time."

Caius Caesar was the grandson of Caesar Augustus, who adopted him in hopes that he would be his heir, but Caius died in 4 C.E. and Augustus died in 14 C.E.

Apicius spent his fortune on pleasure; when he had spent most of his money, he committed suicide.

Sabinus said:

"And now, the second face of the whole world, the partner of the Empire, has his image reared equal with the image of Tiberius, borne in ensigns — military standards."

Sejanus' effigy was displayed in the center of military camps, where the ensigns were stored.

Sabinus continued:

"Sejanus commands and disposes every important, dignified office.

"Centurions, Tribunes, heads of provinces, Praetors, and Consuls, all that heretofore Rome's general suffrage — collective vote — gave, is now his to sell."

A Centurion was a military officer who commanded a century: a unit of Roman soldiers.

Sabinus continued:

"The gain, or rather spoil, of all the earth, one man, and his family, receives."

Silius said, "He has recently made him a strength, too, in an exceptional way, by reducing all the Praetorian bands into one camp, which he commands, after alleging that the soldiers, because of living loose and scattered, fell to debauchery, and that if any sudden attack should be attempted, their united strength would be far more than if the bands of guards were severed and divided into smaller bands, and their life more strict if they were more removed and distant from the city."

From 14 C.E. until a little before his death, Sejanus was Prefect of the Praetorian Guard, aka the Roman imperial bodyguard, which also policed the city of Rome. They had been stationed in various places, but he consolidated them into one camp, which gave him many soldiers to quickly command. His excuses were that the soldiers were prone to dissolute behavior when in widely separated locations, and there would be more discipline if they were consolidated; in addition, he said that they would be a more powerful force if they were all together. The new camp was located outside, but near, Rome.

Sabinus said:

"Where now he builds what kind of forts he pleases, is heard to court the soldier by his name, woos, feasts the chiefest men of action, whose needs, not loves, compel them to be his.

"And, although he never has been liberal by nature, yet to his own dark ends he's most profuse and lavish and letting fly he does not care what toward his ambition."

"Does he yet have ambition?" Arruntius asked. "Is there any step in state that can make him higher? Or more? Or is there anything that he is, except less?"

"Nothing, but Emperor," Silius said.

Sejanus was the second most important man in the Roman Empire. The only higher man and position was Emperor.

"I hope that Tiberius will keep the name of Emperor, howsoever he has foregone the dignity and power," Arruntius said.

Tiberius preferred a quiet life to the burdens of being Emperor.

"To be sure, while he lives," Silius said.

"And when Tiberius is dead, the Emperorship comes to Drusus Senior," Arruntius said. "Should he fail, aka die, the Emperorship comes to the brave offspring of Germanicus, and they are three: Is that too many for him to have a plot upon?"

The three sons of Germanicus were Nero, Drusus Junior, and Caligula. When Tiberius died, the four men in line to succeed him were his son, Drusus Senior, and the three sons of Tiberius' nephew and adopted son: Germanicus.

In order for Sejanus to succeed Tiberius as Emperor, he would have to kill the four men in line ahead of him. If he wanted the deaths to appear to be natural, they would have to be spaced out.

"I do not know the heart of Sejanus' designs; but surely the face — the outward appearance — of his designs and plans looks farther than the present," Sabinus said.

Arruntius said:

"By the gods, if I could guess he had but such a thought, my sword should cleave him down from head to heart, but I would find it out; and with my hand I'd hurl his panting brain about the air, in mites as small as atoms, to undo the knotted bed —"

The "knotted bed" was Sejanus' immoral plans.

A knot is a jumble of ropes. Arruntius may be comparing Sejanus' thoughts to a nest of snakes or to the intricately woven threads of plots.

"You're observed, Arruntius," Sabinus said. "You're being watched."

Some of Sejanus' clients were watching him.

Arruntius said, "Death! I dare tell him so, and all his spies."

He turned to Sejanus's clients and said, "You, sir, I would — do you look? And you?"

Sabinus said to Arruntius, "Forbear. Don't do this."

Satrius and Eudemus entered the scene. They stood apart from the Germanicans: Sabinus, Arruntius, Silius, and Cordus.

Satrius was a follower of Sejanus, and he was the go-between for Eudemus and Sejanus. Eudemus was the physician of Livia, the wife of Drusus Senior. Eudemus was bribing Sejanus in order to become a Tribune.

Satrius said to Eudemus, "Sejanus will quickly be here. Let's walk a turn. You're musing, Eudemus?"

Cautious, Eudemus said to Satrius, "Not I, sir."

He said to himself, "I wonder why Sejanus should mark me out for attention so! Well, may Jove and Apollo form it for the best."

Jove (aka Jupiter) and Apollo were Roman gods.

Satrius said:

"Your fortune's made for you now, Eudemus, if you can just lay hold upon the means."

The means is service.

Satrius continued:

"Do but observe his mood, and — believe it — he's the noblest Roman, where he takes —"

Sejanus entered the scene, and Satrius said, "Here comes His Lordship."

"Now, good Satrius," Sejanus said.

"This is the gentleman, my lord," Satrius said.

"Is he?" Sejanus asked.

He said to Eudemus, "Give me your hand. We must be more acquainted. Report, sir, has spoken out about your skill and learning, and I am glad I have so needful cause (however in itself painful and hard) to make me known to so great ability."

He then said to Satrius, to get him out of the way, "Look, who's that, Satrius?"

Taking the hint, Satrius exited.

Sejanus then said to Eudemus, "I have a grief — an injury — sir, that will desire your help. Your name's Eudemus?"

"Yes," Eudemus said.

"Sir?" Sejanus said.

Sejanus wanted Eudemus to be more respectful to him, which Eudemus immediately recognized and obliged.

Eudemus said, "It is, My Lord."

"I hear that you are the physician to Livia, the princess?" Sejanus said.

"I minister unto her, my good lord," Eudemus replied.

"You minister to a royal lady, then," Sejanus said.

"She is royal, my lord, and fair," Eudemus replied.

Sejanus said:

"Being fair — beautiful — is understood of all their sex, who are, or would be so.

"Those who would be fair, cosmetic treatment soon can make them so.

"For those who are fair, their beauties fear no colors."

Colors are 1) makeup, and 2) battle flags.

"Your Lordship is conceited," Eudemus said.

In this context, the word "conceited" means "full of conceits, aka ideas," aka "witty."

Sejanus said:

"Sir, you know it. And I can, if necessary, deliver a learned lecture on this and other secrets.

"Please tell me, what other ladies, besides Livia, do you have as your patients?"

Eudemus answered, "Many, my good lord. The great Augusta, Urgulania, Mutilia Prisca, and Plancina, many different —"

Augusta was the mother of Tiberius.

Urgulania was one of Augusta's best friends.

Mutilia Prisca was another intimate friend of Augusta's.

Plancina, another of Augusta's friends, was the wife of Gnaeus Calpurnius Piso. Plancina and Piso were thought to have poisoned Germanicus and killed him.

Sejanus interrupted, "— and all of these tell you the particulars of every different grief? How first it grew, and then increased? What action caused that? What passion caused that? And they answer to each point — each question — that you will put to them?"

"If they did not, my lord, we doctors would not know how to prescribe the remedies," Eudemus said.

"Bah, you're a subtle, cunning nation of persons, you physicians! And you are grown to be the only cabinets — the only repositories— in court of ladies' privacies and secrets."

"Cabinets" are private apartments or boudoirs.

"Privacies" can be "intimacies" and/or "private parts."

Sejanus then asked, "Indeed, which of these is the most pleasant and amusing lady, in her physic?"

"Physic" is "medicine." It can include such practices as taking cathartics or purgatives. "Physic" can also mean "healthy practices."

Eudemus hesitated. Physicians know things that their patients would not like to be made public knowledge.

Sejanus said, "Come, you are modest now."

"It is fitting for me to be modest, my lord," Eudemus said.

Sejanus said:

"Why, sir, I do not ask you about their urines.

"I do not ask you whose urine smells most like violets as a result of using violets in herbal medicines, or whose excrement is best, or who makes the hardest faces on her toilet-stool during a difficult defecation.

"I do not ask you which lady sleeps with her own face a-nights, which lady takes her teeth off with her clothes, in court, or which lady takes off her hair, or which lady takes off her complexion, and in which box she puts it.

"These would be questions that might, perhaps, have put your gravity to some defense of blush. But I inquired, which was the wittiest, merriest, most wanton?"

The word "wanton" can mean 1) "playful," or 2) "lustful."

Sejanus continued:

"I made harmless interrogatories and asked questions that are simply harmless whims."

Manipulative people will often test other people in small ways to see if those people can be manipulated in big ways.

He then asked:

"I think Augusta should be most perverse and unreasonable by temperament?"

"She's so, my lord," Eudemus said.

Yes, Eudemus can be manipulated.

"I knew it," Sejanus said. "And Mutilia is the most jocund?"

"It is very true, my lord," Eudemus said.

Sejanus said:

"And why would you conceal this from me, now?

"Come, what about Livia? I know she's quick and quaintly spirited, and she will have strange thoughts when she's at leisure.

"She tells them all to you?"

"Quaintly" can mean "elegantly" or "cleverly," but in Ben Jonson's society, the word "quaint" also meant "cunt."

A "strange woman" can be a promiscuous woman.

Eudemus said, "My noblest lord, there is no man alive and breathing in the Empire or on earth whom I would be ambitious to serve in any act that may preserve my honor before Your Lordship."

If Eudemus were to answer Sejanus' prying questions, Eudemus would NOT be preserving his own honor.

Sejanus said:

"Sir, you can lose no honor by trusting anything — any information — to me. The coarsest act done to my service I can so reward in such a way that all the world shall style it honorable.

"People's idle, foolish, virtuous definitions keep honor poor, and are as scorned as vain;

"Those deeds breathe honor that do suck in gain."

According to Sejanus, honorable deeds are those that bring you wealth.

Eudemus objected: "But, my good lord, if I should thus betray the private counsels of my patient, and the private counsels of a lady of her high place and worth, what might Your Lordship — who soon are to trust me with your own private counsels — judge about my trustworthiness?"

Soon, if Sejanus were to make Eudemus his physician, Sejanus would entrust Eudemus with his own secrets. If Eudemus were to tell Sejanus the secrets of Eudemus' patients, wouldn't Sejanus think that Eudemus would tell other people the secrets of Sejanus?

Sejanus said:

"I would judge your trustworthiness to be only the best, I swear.

"Say now that I should utter to you my illness, and with it the true cause: that my illness is love, and love for Livia; if you should tell her this, should she suspect your faith? I wish you could tell me as much from her; see if my brain could be turned mistrustful."

Sejanus was claiming to be lovesick for Livia, a married woman.

Eudemus said, "Happily, my lord, I could in time tell you as much, and more, as long as I might safely promise but the first to her from you."

The word "happily" can mean "perhaps."

Sejanus said, "You may tell it as safely, my Eudemus (I now dare call thee so) as I have put the secret into thee."

Sejanus had been using the formal "you" to refer to Eudemus, but now he used the familiar "thee," indicating that he was regarding Eudemus as a friend.

Eudemus said, "My lord —"

"Don't protest," Sejanus said. "Thy looks are vows to me; use only speed, and, if you just move and persuade her with Sejanus' love, thou are a man made to make Consuls. Go."

A man made to make Consuls is a powerful man: He can decide who is to be Consul, which in itself is an important position.

"My lord, I'll promise you a private meeting this day, together with her," Eudemus said.

"Can thou?" Sejanus asked.

"Yes," Eudemus said.

"The place?" Sejanus asked.

"My gardens, to where I shall fetch Your Lordship," Eudemus said.

Sejanus said:

"Let me adore my Aesculapius!"

Aesculapius is the god of medicine.

Sejanus continued:

"Why, this indeed is physic, and outspeaks — is more significant than — the knowledge of cheap drugs, or any use that can be made out of it! More comforting than all your opiates, juleps, apozems, magistral syrups, or —"

Opiates, juleps, apozems, and magistral syrups are different kinds of medicine.

Sejanus broke off his words and then continued:

"Begone, my friend, not barely styled, but created so. Expect things greater than thy largest hopes to overtake thee. Fortune shall be taught to know how ill she has deserved, thus long to come behind thy wishes. Go, and be successful."

Lady Fortune had been slow in answering Eudemus' prayers, but Sejanus would make sure that Eudemus' wishes were now quickly answered. Sejanus was promising that he was not making an empty promise but would do what he said he would do.

Eudemus, who had just agreed to arrange a meeting between Sejanus and a married woman, exited.

People who arrange such meetings are sometimes called panders.

Sejanus, who had just manipulated Eudemus, said to himself:

"Ambition makes more trusty slaves than does need. These fellows —
doctors — by the favor of their art and skill, have always the means to tempt,
and they have often the power."

Sejanus was going to use Eudemus to tempt Livia. As a doctor, Eudemus
knew Livia's secrets, and so he had inside information on what would tempt her.

Eudemus was ambitious, as shown by his wanting to be a Tribune, and so
he would make a trusty slave to Sejanus.

Sejanus continued:

"If Livia will be now corrupted, then thou have the way, Sejanus, to work
out the secrets of him, who, thou know, endures and tolerates thee not. I mean
to find out the secrets of her husband, Drusus Senior, and to work against them.

"Prosper it, Pallas, thou who betters wit;

"For Venus has the smallest share in it."

Pallas Athena is a warrior goddess, while Venus is the goddess of sexual
passion. Sejanus was more concerned about killing Drusus Senior than he was
about getting an orgasm. Seducing Livia was simply a means to a more immoral
end.

Because Pallas Athena is also the goddess of wisdom, she can better wit, aka
intelligence. Venus, as the goddess of sexual passion, has much less to do with
reason.

Tiberius and Drusus Senior, attended by Haterius, Latiaris, Satrius, Natta,
etc., entered the scene.

A man knelt before Tiberius, who said:

"We will not endure and tolerate these flatteries.

"Let him stand.

"Our empire, ensigns, axes, rods, and state don't take away our human
nature from us.

'Look up at us like a man, and fall before the gods."

Axes and rods make up the *fasces*, symbol of the Emperor's power.

Tiberius wanted his followers to look at him as the man — not god — he
was, but also to look up to him.

Suetonius wrote about Tiberius' aversion to flattery. In Alexander
Thomson's translation:

*He had such an aversion to flattery, that he would never suffer any senator
to approach his litter, as he passed the streets in it, either to pay him a civility,*

or upon business. And when a man of consular rank, in begging his pardon for some offence he had given him, attempted to fall at his feet, he started from him in such haste, that he stumbled and fell. If any compliment was paid him, either in conversation or a set speech, he would not scruple to interrupt and reprimand the party, and alter what he had said. Being once called "lord," by some person, he desired that he might no more be affronted in that manner. When another, to excite veneration, called his occupations "sacred," and a third had expressed himself thus: "By your authority I have waited upon the senate," he obliged them to change their phrases; in one of them adopting persuasion, instead of "authority," and in the other, laborious, instead of "sacred."

"How like a god speaks Caesar!" Sejanus said.

This, of course, was flattery. One way to flatter someone is to say that that person does not like flattery. And, of course, Sejanus was comparing Tiberius to the gods.

Arruntius said to Cordus, Silius, and Sabinus:

"There, observe! Tiberius can endure that second supporter who flatters him secondly — that's no flattery — ha!

"Oh, what is it proud slime will not believe of his own worth, to hear it equally praised thus with the gods!"

"He did not hear what Sejanus said, sir," Cordus said.

Arruntius said:

"He did not?

"Tut, he must not; we think meanly and ignobly.

"It is your most courtly, known confederacy to have your private parasite redeem what he in public subtlety will lose to making him a name."

In other words: It is most courtly to have a flatterer restore a name privately that the Emperor or other high-ranking person declines publicly in order to please the citizens. Tiberius was saying that he was not a god, but Sejanus was comparing him to the gods.

Silius will soon say that Tiberius has a secret love of flattery although he rejects flattery publicly.

Haterius gave Tiberius some letters and began, "Right mighty lord —"

Using the majestic plural, Tiberius interrupted and said, "We must stop up our ears against these assaults of charming and enchanted tongues; we ask that you use no longer these contumelies to us; don't call us either 'lord,' or 'mighty.'

We profess ourself to be the servant of the Senate, and we are proud to enjoy them as our good, just, and favoring lords."

The noun "contumely" means "insulting language." Tiberius considered flattery directed toward himself to be insulting language.

Cordus said to Arruntius, Sabinus, and Silius, "Splendidly dissembled!"

The word "dissimulation" means "concealment of one's thoughts."

Earlier, Sabinus had said about Tiberius: "Often Tiberius has been heard, while leaving the court, to cry, 'O race of men, prepared for servitude!'"

Tiberius did not highly regard all of the Senators and other members of the court.

Tiberius was very capable of saying one thing but doing the opposite.

Arruntius said, "Princelike, to the life."

Sabinus said:

"When power, which may command, so much descends,

"Their bondage, whom it stoops to, it intends."

Sabinus believed that Tiberius was manipulating the Senators and the people listening to him.

Tiberius asked Haterius, "From where come these letters?"

"From the Senate," Haterius answered.

"I see," Tiberius said.

Latiaris gave him more letters.

Tiberius asked, "From where come these?"

"From the Senate, too," Latiaris said.

"Are the Senators sitting now?" Tiberius asked.

"They await thy answer, Caesar," Latiaris said.

The Senators were waiting for his answer to the letters.

Silius and the other Germanicans continued to talk privately among themselves.

Silius said:

"If this man just had a mind allied to his words, how blest a fate it would be to us, and Rome! We could not imagine that state for which we would exchange Tiberius' state, although the aim were our old liberty."

In other words: If Tiberius' actions matched his words, we cannot imagine another government that we would exchange for his government, even if the new government were to give us back our old liberty.

Silius continued:

"The ghosts of those who fell for that would grieve that their bodies lived not now, so that they could again serve. Men are deceived who think there can be thrall — bondage — beneath a virtuous prince. Wished-for liberty never looks lovelier than that which is under such a crown.

"But when his grace is merely only lip-good — and not good in deeds — and that no longer than he airs himself abroad in public, there to seem to shun the strokes and stripes of flatterers, which within his true character are lechery unto him —"

To some people, the strokes and stripes of flattery are sexually pleasurable.

Silius continued:

"— and so feed his brutish sense with their afflicting sound, as, dead to virtue, he permits himself to be carried like a pitcher, by the ears, to every act of vice."

In other words: He can be easily manipulated by flattery to do evil.

Silius continued:

"This is a case that deserves our fear and presages the close and secret approach of blood and tyranny.

"Flattery is midwife to princes' rage, and nothing sooner helps bring forth a tyrant than that, and whisperers' grace, who have the time, the place, the power to make all men offenders."

Arruntius said:

"Tiberius should be told this, and he should be advised to dissemble with fools and blind men. We who know the evil should hunt the palace-rats, or give them poison, frighten away from here these worse than ravens. Flatterers devour the living, where ravens just prey upon the dead.

"Tiberius shall be told it."

A proverb stated, "Flatterers are worse than crows."

Sabinus said:

"Wait, Arruntius, we must wait for our opportunity, and practice what is fitting, as well as what is needful.

"It is not safe to approach by force a sovereign's ear;

"Princes hear well, if they at all will hear."

Arruntius replied:

"Ha! Do you say so? Well.

"In the meantime, Jove — don't say that I am doing this, but I am calling upon thee now —

"Of all wild beasts, preserve me from a tyrant.

"And of all tame beasts, preserve me from a flatterer!"

"It is well prayed," Silius said.

Tiberius said to Haterius:

"Deliver to the lords this voice and message:

"We are their servant, and it is fitting that a good and honest prince, whom they, out of their bounty, have instructed and provided with so enlarged and absolute a power should owe the performance of it to their service, and to the good of all and the good of every citizen.

"Nor shall it ever make us regret to have wished the Senate just and favoring lords to us, since their free loves yield no less defense to a prince's state than his own innocence.

"Say then, there can be nothing in their thought that shall fail to please us, which has pleased them. Our suffrage shall rather anticipate and come before than stay behind their wills.

"It is empire — supreme power — to obey where such, so great, so grave, so good, determine."

Tiberius explained why he had allowed one temple to be erected to him but would not allow another temple to be erected to him:

"Yet for the suit of Spain to erect a temple in honor of our mother and ourself, we must (with pardon of the Senate) not assent to.

"Their Lordships may object that we did not deny the same recent request to the Asian cities. We desire that our defense for allowing that should be known in these brief reasons, with our after-purpose — our intention for the future.

"Since deified Augustus did not stop a temple to him from being built at Pergamum in honor of himself and sacred Rome, we, who have all observed all the deeds and words observed of Augustus always in place of laws, we rather followed that pleasing precedent because, with our own reverence, the Senate's reverence also there was joined.

"But as to have once received it may deserve the winning of pardon, so to be adored with the continued style and note — reputation or name — of gods through all the provinces would be wild ambition, and no less pride.

Yea, even Augustus' name should early vanish, should it be profaned with such promiscuous flatteries."

Tiberius then explained how he wished to be regarded:

"As for our part, we here protest it, and we desire that posterity should know this: We are mortal, and we can do only the deeds of men. It would be glory enough if we could be truly a prince. And they shall add abounding grace to our memory who shall report us worthy of our forefathers, taking care of your affairs, constant and standing firm in dangers, and not afraid of any private frown when acting for the public good. These things shall be to us temples and statues, reared in your minds, the fairest and most enduring imagery.

"For those of stone or brass, if they become odious in judgment of posterity, are more contemned as dying sepulchers than taken for living monuments."

Tiberius then explained what he wanted from the gods and men:

"We then make here our suit, alike to gods and men.

"Our suit to the gods is to, until the end of our life, inspire us with a free and quiet mind, discerning both divine and human laws.

"Our suit to men is to vouchsafe us after death an honorable mention, and fair praise to accompany our actions and our name.

"The rest of greatness princes may command, and therefore may neglect; they should, without being satisfied, pursue only a long, lasting, high, and happy memory.

"Contempt of fame — reputation — begets contempt of virtue."

"Splendid!" Natta said.

"Most divine!" Satrius said.

"The oracles have ceased to speak, so that only Caesar might speak with their tongue," Sejanus said.

Oracles were believed to speak with the voice of gods. For example, the oracle at Delphi spoke with the voice of Apollo.

The oracles, including the oracle at Delphi, were said to have ceased speaking after the birth of Christ.

Sejanus said blasphemously that now the oracles are said to have stopped speaking on account of Tiberius, who speaks god-like words.

Arruntius said to Cordus, Silius, and Sabinus, "Let me be gone! This is most perceived and open!"

He did not like the flattery of Tiberius that he was hearing. He also did not like what he considered to be manipulative words by Tiberius.

Cordus said to Arruntius, "Stay."

Arruntius said to Cordus, Silius, and Sabinus, "Why? To hear more cunning, and to hear more fine words with their sound flattered, before their sense is meant?"

Tiberius said:

"Their choice of Antium, there to place the gift vowed to the goddess for our mother's health, we want the Senate to know we fairly like."

The gift was a statue of Fortuna Equestris, which was donated by the Roman equestrian order and placed in Fortuna's temple at Actium. The gift was an offering to Lady Fortune asking for Augusta to have good health.

Tiberius continued:

"We also like the Senate's permission to Marcus Lepidus to repair the Aemilian place, and to restore those monuments."

Lepidus wanted to improve the Basilica of Paulus at his own expense.

Tiberius continued:

"We like their grace, too, in the confining of Silanus to the other isle Cythera, at the suit of his religious sister. This grace much commends their wisdom and policy, being so tempered with their mercy."

Silanus was supposed to be exiled on an island that was barren, but his religious sister had asked that he instead be exiled on the island of Cynthus (called Cythera here).

Tiberius continued:

"But, for the honors that they have decreed to our Sejanus, to raise his statue in Pompey's Theater — whose ruining fire his vigilance and labor kept restrained in that one loss —"

Pompey's Theater had been destroyed by a fire. Tiberius gave credit to Sejanus for keeping the destruction restricted to one place instead of spreading through the city, and the Senators voted for a statue of Sejanus to be placed in the restored theater.

Tiberius praised both the Senate and Sejanus:

"— they have therein outgone their own great wisdoms by their skillful choice and placing of their generous bounties on a man whose merit more adorns the dignity than that dignity can adorn him, and gives a benefit in taking, greater than it can receive.

"Blush not, Sejanus, thou great aid of Rome, associate of our labors, our chief helper.

"Let us not do violence to thy unfeigned modesty by attempting to give thee thy deserved praise, for we cannot do more than attempt to do so, since there's no voice that can undertake it.

"No man here receive our speeches as hyperboles, for we are as far from flattering our friend, let malicious envy know, as from the need to flatter.

"Nor let them ask the reasons of our praise.

"Princes have always their grounds reared with themselves, above the poor low flats of common men, and whoever will search the reasons of their acts must stand on equal bases."

High princes stand on high grounds, while common men stand on a lower firmament. The "high grounds" can be justifying motives.

Tiberius concluded:

"Lead, let's go! Our loves will go to the Senate."

Tiberius, Sejanus, Haterius, Latiaris, Satrius, Natta, etc., exited.

Arruntius shouted at the departing Tiberius, "Caesar!"

Holding Arruntius back, Sabinus said, "Peace! Be quiet!"

Cordus said, "Great Pompey's Theater was never ruined until now that proud Sejanus has a statue reared on its ashes."

Arruntius said, "Place the shame of soldiers above the best of generals? Crack the world, and bruise and crush the name of Romans into dust, before we behold it!"

According to Arruntius, the best of generals is Pompey, and the shame of soldiers is Sejanus.

"Check your passion," Silius said. "Lord Drusus tarries."

Drusus Senior approached Arruntius, Cordus, Satrius, and Sabinus.

Drusus Senior, who greatly disliked Sejanus, said:

"Is my father mad?

"Weary of life and rule, lords? Thus to heave an idol up with praise? Make him his mate? His partner in the Empire?"

"O good prince!" Arruntius said.

Drusus Senior said, "Allow him statues? Titles? Honors? Such as he himself refuses?"

"Bravo, brave Drusus!" Arruntius said.

Drusus Senior said, "The first ascents to sovereignty are hard, but once entered, there never lacks either means or ministers to help the aspirer on."

"True, gallant Drusus," Arruntius said.

Drusus Senior said, "We must shortly pray to Modesty that he — Sejanus — will rest contented —"

Modesty is the goddess Pudicitia.

"Aye, where he is, and not write Emperor," Arruntius said.

Sejanus, Satrius, Latiaris, and some of Sejanus' clients entered the scene. They took no notice at first of Drusus Senior and the Germanicans.

Sejanus said to his clients, "There is your bill, and yours. Bring your man. I have interceded for you, too, Latiaris."

Bills are official documents. Apparently, these bills were letters of appointment to positions.

Sejanus then walked into and bumped Drusus Senior.

"What!" Drusus Senior said, "Is your vast greatness grown so blindly bold that you will walk over us?"

"Why, then give way," Sejanus said.

Drusus Senior said, "Give way, Colossus?"

The Colossus of Rhodes was a huge statue. Drusus Senior was accusing Sejanus of carelessly walking as if he were a mobile but blindly bold huge statue. Sejanus' hugeness lay in his ambition and power.

"Do you lift your hand against us?" Drusus Senior said. "Do you advance yourself against us? Take that!"

Drusus Senior struck Sejanus.

"Good! Splendid! Excellent brave prince!" Arruntius said.

Drusus Senior said to Sejanus, "Nay, come, approach."

He then drew his sword and said:

"What! Do you stand away from us? Do you gaze at us with wonder? It looks too full of death for thy cold spirits.

"Avoid my eye, dull camel, or my sword shall make thy bravery and finery fitter for a grave than for a triumph. I'll raise a statue of your own bulk; but it shall be on the cross, where I will nail your pride at breadth and length, and crack those sinews, which are yet but stretched with your swollen fortune's rage."

Crucifixion was an ignominious death.

"A noble prince!" Arruntius said.

The spectators who supported Drusus Senior all cried, "A Castor, a Castor, a Castor, a Castor!"

Castor was a famous gladiator.

Everyone except Sejanus exited.

Sejanus said to himself:

"He who is moved with such wrong but can bear it through with patience and an even mind knows how to turn it back.

"Wrath, covered, carries fate and achieves revenge.

"Revenge is lost, if I express my hate.

"What was my intrigue recently, I'll now pursue as my deadly justice. This has changed my intrigue and made its goal a deadly revenge."

At this point in Ben Jonson's play, a Chorus of Musicians performed.

CHAPTER 2

— 2.1 —

Sejanus, Livia, and Eudemus talked together.

Sejanus said to Eudemus, "Physician, thou are worthy of a province for the great favors done to our loves. And, except that Livia — greatest among the great — bears a part in the requital of thy services, I should alone despair of any adequate way to give them worthy satisfaction."

Livia said, "Eudemus, I will see to it that you shall receive a fit and full reward for your large merit."

She then said, "But for this potion we intend to give to Drusus Senior — who is no longer our husband now — whom shall we choose as the most apt and capable instrument to administer it to him?"

The potion was poison.

"I say Lygdus," Eudemus said.

"Lygdus?" Sejanus asked. "Who's he?"

Livia answered, "He is a eunuch whom Drusus Senior loves and respects."

"Aye, and he is his cup-bearer," Eudemus said.

In Ben Jonson's society, the words "Ganymede" and "cup-bearer" were then-slang for "catamite," aka the "bottom" in gay anal sex. In mythology, Jupiter, the king of the gods, may have had a homosexual relationship with Ganymede, who was Jupiter's cupbearer.

Sejanus said, "Don't name a second person to do this. If Drusus loves and respects him, and he has that position of cup-bearer, we cannot think of a fitter person to administer the poison."

Eudemus said, "True, my lord, for free access and trust are two main aids."

Lygdus had access to the presence of Drusus Senior, and Drusus Senior trusted him.

"Skillful physician!" Sejanus said.

Livia said, "But he must be wrought and persuaded to the undertaking with some elaborate art."

"Is he ambitious?" Sejanus asked.

"No," Livia said.

"Or covetous?" Sejanus asked.

"Neither," Livia answered.

"Yet gold is a good general charm," Eudemus said.

"What is he, then?" Sejanus asked.

"Indeed, only wanton, light," Livia answered.

"What! Is he young? And fair?" Sejanus asked.

"He is a delicate youth," Eudemus answered.

Sejanus said: "Send him to me. I'll work on him."

He then worked on Livia:

"Royal lady, though I have loved you long, and with that height of zeal and duty (like the fire, which the more it mounts, the more it trembles), thinking nothing could add to the fervor that your eye had kindled, yet, now I see your wisdom, judgment, strength, quickness, and will to apprehend the means to your own good and greatness, I protest myself thoroughly purified, and I have turned into all flame because of my affection and love for you.

"Such a spirit as yours was not created to be the idle second, aka follower, to a poor flash — fop — as Drusus, but to shine bright as the moon among the lesser lights and share the sovereignty of all the world.

"Then Livia triumphs in her proper sphere, when she and her Sejanus shall divide the name of Caesar, and Augusta's star should be dimmed by the glory of a brighter beam.

"At that time Agrippina's fires will be quite extinct, and the scarcely seen Tiberius will borrow all his little light from us, whose folded arms — mutual embrace — shall make one perfect orb."

Augusta was the mother of Tiberius, and Agrippina was the widow of Germanicus.

Knocking sounded on the door.

Sejanus said:

"Who's that? Eudemus, look. Isn't it Drusus Senior?"

"Lady, do not fear."

"Not I, my lord," Livia said. "My fear and love of him left me at once."

Sejanus said, "Illustrious lady! Wait —"

Eudemus entered while saying to someone, "I'll tell His Lordship."

"Who is it, Eudemus?" Sejanus asked.

Eudemus answered, "One of Your Lordship's servants, who brings you word that the Emperor Tiberius has sent for you."

"Oh!" Sejanus said. "Where is he?"

He then said to Livia, "With your fair permission, dear princess. I'll just ask a question, and return."

He went out.

Eudemus said to Livia, "Fortunate princess! How you are blest in the fruition — the possession and enjoyment — of this unequalled man, this soul of Rome, the life of the Empire, and the voice of Caesar's world!"

Livia responded, "So blessed, my Eudemus, as to know the bliss I have, with what I ought to owe the means — that is you, Eudemus — that wrought it. How do I look today?"

"Excellently clear, believe it," Eudemus said. "This same fucus was well laid on."

Fucus is a kind of face makeup.

"I think it is not white here," Livia said, looking in a mirror.

"Lend me your scarlet cloth, lady," Eudemus said. "It is the sun that has given some little taint unto the ceruse."

Ceruse is white lead (or another foundation cream), used as a cosmetic. It was sensitive to light.

Painting her cheeks, Eudemus said, "You should have used some of the white oil I gave you."

Eudemus was a cosmetician as well as a medical doctor.

He then said, "Sejanus, for your love! His very name commands above Cupid, or his shafts —"

The god Cupid shot arrows that caused people to fall in love, but according to Eudemus, Sejanus had more power than Cupid and his arrows.

"Nay, now you've made it worse," Livia said.

Did her words refer only to the makeup?

Eudemus said:

"I'll fix it right away —

"And, Sejanus' name, just pronounced, is a sufficient charm against all rumor; and of absolute power to satisfy for any lady's honor."

Eudemus prepared more cosmetic.

"What are you doing now, Eudemus?" Livia asked.

Eudemus said:

"Making a light fucus, to give you a touch-up.

"Honored Sejanus! What act (though never so abnormal, and immoderate) exists but that a title will at least carry it off, if it does not expiate and atone for it?"

If you are a VIP like Sejanus is, you can get away with any act. So said Eudemus.

"Here, good physician," Livia said.

Eudemus said:

"I like this undertaking to preserve the love of such a man, who does not come every hour to greet the world. It is now well, lady, that you should use some of the dentifrice I prescribed you, too, to clear and clean your teeth, and the prepared pomatum, to smooth the skin."

A pomatum is a scented ointment for the skin.

Eudemus continued:

"A lady cannot be too careful of her shape and beauty, who always would hold the heart of such a person, made her captive, as you have his — who, to endear him more in your clear eye, has put away his wife, the trouble and vexation of his bed and your delights, fair Apicata, and made spacious room to your new pleasures."

One reason for Sejanus to divorce Apicata, his wife and the mother of his three children, and then marry Livia is that Livia was the sister of Germanicus, and Germanicus was the nephew and adopted son of Tiberius. Such a marriage could increase Sejanus' chances of becoming Emperor.

Livia responded, "Haven't we given Sejanus a sufficient return for that, with our hatred of Drusus Senior, and by revealing all of Drusus' secrets?"

Eudemus said:

"Yes, and wisely, lady.

"The ages that succeed and stand far off to gaze at your high prudence shall admire and reckon it an act beyond the comprehension of your sex. It has that rare — splendid and remarkable — appearance.

"Some will think your fortune could not yield a deeper sounding than mixed with Drusus Senior; but when they shall hear that and the thunder of Sejanus meet — Sejanus, whose high name strikes the stars, and rings about the concave — the vault of heaven — great Sejanus, whose glories, style, and titles are appropriate to himself, the often iterating of Sejanus — they then will lose their thoughts and be ashamed to take acquaintance of them."

Sejanus returned and said, "I must make a rude departure, lady. Caesar sends to me to come to him with all his haste both of command and prayer."

Hmm. It seems that Caesar's high name strikes the stars, and rings about the concave — the vault of heaven. It is certain that Sejanus quickly obeys Tiberius' command to come to him.

Sejanus continued saying to Livia, "Be resolute in our plot; you have my soul, as certainly yours as it is my body's."

He then said to Eudemus:

"And, wise physician, so prepare the poison in such a way that you may blame the subtle operation upon some natural disease of his.

"Send your eunuch to me."

The poison Eudemus would prepare would be intended to make Drusus Senior's death look as if it were due to natural causes.

Sejanus said to Livia, "I kiss your hands, glory of ladies, and I commend my love to your best faith and memory."

Livia responded:

"My lord, I shall but repeat and return your words to you.

"Farewell.

"Yet, remember this for your heed: Drusus Senior does not love you. You know what I have told you: His designs and plans are full of grudge and danger.

"We must use more than a common speed."

"Excellent lady, how you do set my blood on fire!" Sejanus said.

Livia said:

"Well, you must go?

"The thoughts that are best are least set forth to show."

Sejanus exited.

"When will you take some medicine, lady?" Eudemus asked.

The medicine may be makeup.

"When I shall have a mind to, Eudemus," Livia said, "but let Drusus' drug be prepared first."

Eudemus said:

"If Lygdus were prepared to act, that's already done: I have it ready.

"And tomorrow morning I'll send you a perfume, first to dissolve and procure sweat, and then prepare a bath to cleanse and clear the skin; in preparation for when, I'll have an excellent new fucus made, resistant against the sun, the rain, or the wind, which you shall blow on your skin in powder form or rub on your skin after the powder is mixed with oil, as you like best, and the fucus will last some fourteen hours.

"This change came timely, lady, for your health, and for restoring your complexion, which Drusus' choler — his hot anger — had almost burnt up. In this, your fortune has prescribed you better medicine than the medical art could do."

Livia said:

"Thanks, good physician. I'll use my fortune — you shall see — with reverence.

"Is my coach ready?"

Eudemus said, "It attends Your Highness."

While waiting to see Tiberius, Sejanus said to himself:

"If this is not revenge, when I have finished and made it perfect, then let Egyptian slaves, Parthians, and barefoot Hebrews brand my face and print my body full of injuries."

Sejanus then addressed Drusus Senior, who was not present, in an apostrophe:

"Thou lost thyself, child-prince Drusus, when thou thought thou could outskip my vengeance, or withstand the power I had to crush thee into air."

Sejanus was using the word "thou" to contemptuously mean Drusus Senior.

Sejanus continued:

"Thy follies now shall taste what kind of man they have provoked, and this thy father's house shall crack in the flame of my incensed and kindled rage whose fury shall admit no shame or moderation.

"Adultery? It is the lightest ill I will commit."

Matthew 5:32 states, "*But I say unto you, That whosoever shall put away his wife, saving for the cause of fornication, causeth her to commit adultery: and whosoever shall marry her that is divorced committeth adultery.*" (King James Version)

Matthew 19:9 states, "*And I say unto you, Whosoever shall put away his wife, except it be for fornication, and shall marry another, committeth adultery: and whoso marrieth her which is put away doth commit adultery.*" (King James Version)

Mark 10:11-12 ((King James Version) states:

11. *And he saith unto them, Whosoever shall put away his wife, and marry another, committeth adultery against her.*

12. *And if a woman shall put away her husband, and be married to another, she committeth adultery.*

Sejanus had put away his wife, although she had not committed fornication.

Sejanus continued his apostrophe to Drusus Senior:

"A race of wicked acts shall flow out of my anger and overspread the world's wide face, which no posterity shall ever approve, nor yet keep silent — things that for their cunning, close, and cruel mark, thy father — Tiberius — would wish his — and shall, perhaps, carry the empty name, but we the prize."

"Emperor" can be an empty name if someone else has the power of an Emperor.

Sejanus then addressed his soul:

"Onward then, my soul, and don't flinch and swerve from thy course. Though heaven drop sulphur — lightning — and hell belch out fire, laugh at the idle terrors.

"Tell proud Jove that between his power and thine there is no odds.

"It was only fear first in the world made gods."

Tiberius and some attendants entered the room.

"Has Sejanus come yet?" Tiberius asked an attendant.

Sejanus said, "He's here, dread Caesar."

Tiberius sat on his throne and ordered his attendants, "Let all depart that chamber, and the next."

He did not want this conversation to be overheard.

His attendants exited, leaving Tiberius and Sejanus alone.

The two would hold a Machiavellian conversation. Possibly, each person was trying to manipulate the other person.

Tiberius said to Sejanus:

"Sit down, my comfort.

"When the master prince of all the world, Sejanus, says he fears, is it not fatal?"

Tiberius was saying that he feared some people and he was asking, Isn't such a fear fatal?

His words, however, could be interpreted as saying that Sejanus was "the master prince of all the world."

Sejanus answered, "Yes, to those whom the master prince fears."

One way not to fear someone was to kill that person.

"And not to him?" Tiberius asked.

"Not if he wisely turns that part of fate he holds first on them," Sejanus said.

"Nature, blood, and laws of kinship forbid that," Tiberius said.

Killing relatives is unnatural and there are laws against murder.

"Do state policy and state concerns forbid it?" Sejanus asked.

State policy and state concerns are often cynical and cunning.

"No," Tiberius said.

"Let the rest of poor scruples and considerations go by, then. Ignore them," Sejanus said. "Statecraft is enough to make the act just, and it is enough to make them guilty."

"Long hate pursues such acts," Tiberius said.

Other people may — make that will — want to avenge an unjust killing.

"Whom hatred frightens, let him not dream on sovereignty," Sejanus said.

Want to remain an Emperor? Kill your enemies, and don't worry about the hatred of the friends and family of those whom you kill.

"Are rites of faith, love, piety, to be trodden down?" Tiberius asked. "Forgotten? And made vain?"

What about love and morality? Should they be trodden down in the service of ambition?

Sejanus said:

"All of them should be, for a crown."

He meant the crown of an Emperor, but a crown is also a piece of money.

Sejanus continued:

"The prince who is ashamed to bear the name of tyrant shall never dare do anything but fear.

"All the command of scepters quite perishes if command begins to cherish religious thoughts:

"Whole empires fall, swayed by those fine, delicate, fastidious respects.

"It is the lawlessness of dark deeds that protects even the most hated states, when no laws resist the sword, and the sword enacts what it wishes."

If you wish to be an Emperor, be prepared to be called a tyrant and be prepared to do the things a tyrant does.

"Yet in that way we may do all things cruelly, not safely," Tiberius said.

"We can do them safely if we do them thoroughly," Sejanus said.

Tiberius asked, "Does Sejanus know yet at whom we point?"

Sejanus replied, "Aye, or else my thought, my sense, or both do err: Is it Agrippina?"

Agrippina was the widow of Germanicus and the granddaughter of Caesar Augustus.

"She, and her proud race," Tiberius said.

He feared not only her, but some of her family members. Her sons could replace him as Emperor before his time.

Sejanus said, "Proud? They are dangerous, Caesar. For in them the father's spirit quickly shoots up. Germanicus lives in their looks, their gait, their form, to upbraid us with his close — secretly arranged — death, if not to revenge the same."

Tiberius was suspected of having arranged the death by poison of Germanicus, his nephew and adopted son.

"The act's not known," Tiberius said.

Tiberius was suspected, but there was no proof.

Sejanus said:

"The act's not proved. But whispering rumor gives 'knowledge and proof' to the jealous — the suspicious — who, rather than admit their ignorance, would believe their own imagination."

A proverb stated, "Jealousy is no judge — nor is suspicion proof."

Sejanus continued:

"It is not safe for the children to draw long breath and live a long time, when they are provoked by a parent's death."

Aristotle's *Rhetoric*, Book 1, Chapter 15, section 14, states, "Foolish is he who, having killed the father, suffers the children to live."

Aristotle was quoting from *Cypria*, a lost epic.

Tiberius said:

"It is as dangerous to make them hence,

"If nothing except their birth is their offence."

If the only thing against them is that they are the children of a foe, then it would be dangerous to remove them.

Sejanus said, "Wait until they strike at Caesar: Then their crime will be enough, but late, and out of time for him to punish."

The alternative would be to let them strike first, but then it will be too late — Tiberius will no longer be Emperor.

"Do they purpose it?" Tiberius said.

Do they intend to depose Tiberius?

Sejanus answered:

"You know, sir, thunder speaks not until it hits."

Lightning strikes first, and then we hear the thunder. Light travels faster than sound.

Tiberius' opponents can strike first, and after they strike, Tiberius will know the outcome.

Sejanus continued:

"Don't be free from anxiety over your safety; none are more swiftly oppressed than they whom over-confidence betrays to rest.

"Let not your daring make your danger such.

"All power's to be feared, where it is too much. The youths are, of themselves, hot, violent, full of great thought; and that male-spirited — ambitious — dame, their mother, Agrippina, neglects no means to promote their interests, by large allowance and approbation, public appearances, increase of train and state, suing for titles. She has them commended with like prayers, like vows, to the same gods, with Caesar."

Tiberius became angry when the high priests added prayers for Nero and Drusus Senior — Agrippina's two oldest sons — to those prayers said for himself.

Sejanus continued:

"Agrippina spends days and nights in banquets and ambitious feasts for the nobility, where Caius Silius, Titius Sabinus, old Arruntius, Asinius Gallus, Furnius, Regulus, and others of that discontented list are the prime guests.

"There, and to these, Agrippina tells whose niece [the Latin *neptis*, which Ben Jonson is translating, means 'granddaughter'; in Ben Jonson's day, the word 'niece' still meant 'granddaughter'] she was, whose daughter she is, and whose wife she was."

Agrippina was the granddaughter of Caesar Augustus, the daughter of Julia (Augustus' daughter), and the wife — now widow — of Germanicus (Tiberius' nephew and adopted son).

Sejanus continued:

"And then she insists that they compare her with Augusta, aye, and prefer her, too, commend her form, and extol her fruitfulness."

Agrippina had three daughters and three sons. The three sons were Nero, Drusus Junior, and Caligula.

In mythology, Niobe was proud of her fruitfulness. She had given birth to six sons and six daughters, and she boasted aloud, "I am more worthy of respect than the goddess Leto, who has given birth to only two children: the twins Apollo and Artemis." Leto's children were angry at the disrespect shown to their mother, and with the anger of the gods, they killed all of Niobe's children in one day by shooting them with arrows. Because of Niobe's pride, Apollo and Diana turned her to stone. Even when she was stone, she grieved for the deaths of her children, and tears trickled down her marble cheeks. Niobe was so proud that she thought she was a better mother than the goddess mother of the god Apollo and the goddess Diana.

Sejanus continued:

"At which speech of hers, a shower of tears falls for the memory of Germanicus, a memory that they blow over and rekindle immediately with windy praise and puffing — puffed-up — hopes of her aspiring, ambitious sons, who, with these hourly gratifications, grow so pleased, and wantonly conceited of themselves that now they do not hesitate to believe they're such as these flatterers give them out to be; and they would be thought to be — more than competitors — the immediate heirs to Tiberius."

Tiberius' Emperorship was not legally hereditary; however, certain people related to him were expected to succeed him.

Sejanus continued:

"While to their thirst of rule they win the rabble, who are always the friend of political change, with hope of future freedom, which on every political change, that rabble greedily, though emptily, expects.

"Caesar, it is age that in all things breeds neglects, and princes who will keep old dignity must not admit too youthful heirs to stand close by — not even their own descendants, except so darkly and humbly, because not in public, set as shadows are in picture, to give height and luster to the princes themselves."

Using the royal plural, Tiberius said, "We will command their rank and haughty thoughts down, and, with a stricter hand than we have yet put forth, we must abate — reduce in size — their retinues, their titles, feasts, and factions."

Sejanus said, "Or else your state — your power — will be abated. But how, sir, will you work?"

"Confine them," Tiberius said. "Imprison them."

Sejanus objected:

"No. They are too great and powerful, and that is too faint a blow to give them now. It would have served at first, when, with the weakest touch, their knot — their tight-knit group — had burst."

A knot is a jumble of ropes. Sejanus may be comparing the knot of enemies to a nest of snakes.

Sejanus continued:

"But now your care and concern must be not to expose and reveal the smallest cord or line — the snares — of your suspicion. For such who know the weight of princes' fear will, when they find themselves discovered, rear their forces, like seen snakes, which otherwise would lie rolled in their circles, close.

"Nothing is more wrathful, daring, or desperate than offenders who have been found out. Where guilt is, rage and courage both abound.

"The course must be to let them still swell up, riot, and surfeit on blind Fortune's cup."

Lady Fortune was often depicted as blindfolded and holding a cornucopia.

Sejanus continued:

"Give them more status and standing, more dignities, more style. Call them to court, to Senate.

"Meanwhile, take from their strength some one or two, or more of the main supporters and partisans — it will frighten the rest — when you have some incidental pretext or side opportunity.

"Thus, with slight sleight you shall disarm them first, and they, in night of — that is, blinded by — their ambition, shall not perceive the lure until, in the trap, they are caught and slain."

Tiberius said:

"We would not kill them if we knew how to save.

"Yet, rather than a throne, it is cheaper to give them a grave."

He then asked:

"Is there no way to bind them by deserts?"

In other words: Is there any way to bind them in loyalty to me by giving them rewards? Can't I do things that deserve their gratitude?

Sejanus said:

"Sir, wolves do change their hair, but not their hearts. While thus your thought is tied to a mean, you neither dare enough, nor act with foresight."

Sejanus was arguing against a middle course on the grounds that it meant not being brave enough and not having foresight enough.

Sejanus continued:

"All modesty is fond; that is, all moderation is foolish. And chiefly where the subject is no less compelled to bear than praise his sovereign's acts."

Tyrants should be tyrants: They need not observe moderation.

Tiberius said:

"We can no longer keep on our mask to thee, our dear Sejanus.

"Thy thoughts are ours, in all things, and we just tested your thoughts' voice, in our designs, which thou has more confirmed us by thy assenting than if heartening Jove had, from his hundred statues, bid us strike, and at the stroke clicked all his marble thumbs."

Tiberius was saying that he had tested Sejanus, and finding that their thoughts were in accord, he would now speak openly to him.

Many marble statues were erected to Jove, aka Jupiter, King of the gods. Imagine Jove's marble thumbs clicking as he judged thumbs-down to all of Tiberius' enemies. In today's popular opinion, thumbs-down in gladiatorial contests meant death.

The thumbs-down sign, however, may mean something different.

Turnebus, in his *Turnebi adversariorum tomi* (1591), a book in Ben Jonson's library, wrote, "To hold the thumb down was, among the Romans, a sign of the greatest approbation." Using this interpretation of the thumbs-down sign, Jupiter would be expressing approval of the working together of Tacitus and Sejanus.

Tiberius continued:

"But who shall first be struck down?"

Sejanus advised:

"First, Caius Silius. He is the most outstanding and most remarkable, and the most dangerous: In power and in reputation, he is equally strong, having commanded an imperial army seven years together, vanquished Sacrovir in Germany, and thence obtained the right to wear the triumphal ornaments."

A triumph — a triumphal procession in Rome — was at this time reserved for the royal family, but victorious generals could be given and wear triumphal ornaments — devices and clothing — that conferred honor on them.

Sejanus continued:

"His steep fall, by how much it does give the weightier crack of sound, will send more wounding terror to the rest, and command them to stand aloof and give more way to our ambushing of the principal actor."

Tiberius asked, "But what about Sabinus?"

Sejanus advised:

"Let him grow a while; his fate is not yet ripe. We must not pluck at all together, lest we catch ourselves.

"And there's Arruntius, too; he only talks.

"But Sosia, Silius' wife, a friend to Agrippina, should be wound in and ensnared now, for she has one Fury in her breast more than hell ever knew; and she should be sent thither — to hell — in time.

"Then there is one Cremutius Cordus, a writing fellow they have got to gather notes of the precedent times and make them into annals — a most tart and bitter spirit, I hear, who, under color — pretense — of praising those precedent times, taxes and accuses the present state, criticizes the men, the actions, leaves no trick, no practice unexamined, draws parallels between the times and the governments. He is a professed champion for the old liberty —"

Tiberius interrupted:

"— a perishing, destructive wretch!

"As if there were that chaos bred in things that laws and liberty would not rather choose to be quite broken and taken hence by us than to have the stain of disgrace to be preserved by such men as the Germanicans.

"Have we the means to make these guilty first?"

Did they have evidence — real or trumped up — to make these people either known to be guilty or seem to be guilty?

Sejanus said:

"Entrust that to me.

"Let Caesar, by his power, just call and cause a formal meeting of the Senate, and I will have substance — evidence or 'evidence' — for an indictment and I will have accusers ready."

"But how?" Tiberius said. "Let us consult."

Sejanus replied:

"We shall misspend the time of action. We should take action rather than talk now."

A proverb stated: "Take not counsel in time of combat."

Sejanus continued:

"Counsels are unfit in business, where all rest is more pernicious than rashness can be. Acts of this close kind thrive more by execution than by advice and consultation.

"There is no lingering in that work begun,

"Which cannot be praised until thoroughly done."

Tiberius replied:

"Our edict shall forthwith command a Senate court of adjudicature. While I can live, I will prevent earth's fury.

"*Εμου θανοντος γαια μιχθητω πυρι.*"

The Greek, translated by W.R. Paton, means, "When I am dead, may earth be overwhelmed with fire."

Tiberius exited.

Postumus entered the scene.

Julius Postumus, who was one of Sejanus' supporters, knew Agrippina well. He was a spy for Sejanus.

He began, "My lord Sejanus —"

"Julius Postumus, come with my wish!" Sejanus said. "I was just wishing for you! What is the news from Agrippina's household?"

"Indeed, there is none," Postumus said. "The members of Agrippina's household all lock up themselves late, and they talk in code. I have not seen a company so changed. Perhaps they had intelligence by augury of our scheming."

Perhaps a fortune teller had told them about Sejanus' plot, which included Postumus.

"When were you there?" Sejanus asked.

"Last night," Postumus said.

"And what guests did you find there?" Sejanus asked

Postumus answered, "Sabinus, Silius — the old list — Arruntius, Furnius, and Gallus."

"Wouldn't these talk?" Sejanus asked.

"They talked only a little, and yet we offered them their choice of topic," Postumus said. "Satrius was with me."

Satrius was a clint of Sejanus.

"Well, their often meeting is guilt enough," Sejanus said. "You forgot to extol the hospitable lady?"

"To extol" means "to raise too high" and "to exaggeratively praise."

People bursting with pride may say things that they would not otherwise say.

Postumus answered, "No, that trick was well put fully to use, and it would have succeeded, too, except that Sabinus coughed a caution out, for Agrippina began to swell with pride."

Sejanus said:

"And may she burst!

"Julius Postumus, I would have you go instantly to the palace of the great Augusta, and, by your kindest friend, get swift access.

"Acquaint her with these meetings. Tell her the words of Silius that you brought me, the other day. Add somewhat to them. Make her understand the danger of Sabinus, and the danger of the times, out of his secretiveness. Attribute to Arruntius words of malice against Caesar; the same, attribute to Gallus. But, above all, attribute words of malice against Caesar to Agrippina.

"Say, as you may truly, that Agrippina's infinite pride, propped with the hopes of her too-fruitful womb, with the devotion of the people opens her mouth wide to swallow sovereignty and have absolute power, and threatens Caesar.

"Stress to Augusta, then, that for her own, great Caesar's, and the public safety, she should stress to Tiberius the urgency of these dangers.

"Caesar is too over-confident, he must be told, and he'll take it best from a mother's tongue.

"Alas! What is it for us to sound and investigate, to explore, watch, oppose, plot, practice, or prevent,

"If he for whom it is so strongly labored shall, out of greatness and free spirit, be supinely negligent?

"Our city's now divided as it was in time of the civil war, and men don't stop themselves from declaring themselves a part of Agrippina's faction."

Civil wars had occurred: one between Julius Caesar and Pompey, and one between Mark Antony/Octavian and Brutus/Cassius. Octavian had then fought Mark Antony. After becoming Emperor, Octavian became Caesar Augustus.

Sejanus continued:

"Every day the faction multiplies, and it will do more if it is not resisted. You can best enlarge and embroider it as you find suitable for your audience.

"Noble Postumus, commend me to your Prisca, and request that she will solicit this great business to earnest and most present execution, with all her utmost credit with Augusta."

Prisca was a woman with whom Postumus was committing adultery. Prisca was close to Augusta.

"I shall not fail in my instructions," Postumus said.

He exited.

Alone, Sejanus said to himself:

"This assistance from Augusta, Tiberius' mother, will well urge our recent design and plot, and spur on Caesar's rage, which otherwise might grow slack.

"The way to put a prince in an alert state of full vigor is to present the shapes of dangers greater than they are, like late or early shadows of the evening or morning, and, sometimes, to feign dangers where there are none, only to make him fear.

"His fear will make him cruel; and once entered into cruelty, he does not easily learn to stop, or spare where he may doubt.

"This have I made my rule, to thrust Tiberius into tyranny, and make him toil to turn aside those blocks and obstacles that I, working alone, could not remove with safety.

"Drusus Senior once gone, Germanicus' three sons would clog my way, but their guards have too much faith to be corrupted, and their mother is known to have too, too unreproved a chastity to be attempted and seduced, as light Livia was."

Sejanus wanted to get rid of Drusus Senior and of Agrippina's three sons (fathered by Germanicus) because they were ahead of him in the expected line of succession to the throne. Her servants, however, were too loyal and honest to be bribed, and Agrippina was a completely chaste woman who could not be seduced.

Sejanus continued:

"I will work then my art on Caesar's fears, as they work on those they fear, until all my obstacles be cleared, and he buries his own state and high position in the ruins of his family and the hatred of all his subjects."

Sejanus wanted to make Tiberius and Agrippina fear each other.

Sejanus continued:

"Then, with my peace and safety, I will rise by making him the public sacrifice."

Sejanus exited.

Satrius and Natta talked together in the house of Agrippina. Both men were clients of Sejanus, who was their patron.

Satrius said, "The Germanicans have grown exceedingly circumspect and wary."

As Postumus had said, the Germanicans had grown cautious.

"They have us in the wind — they smell us," Natta said. "And yet Arruntius cannot contain himself and restrain his tongue."

Arruntius was a Senator of good character.

"Tut, he's not yet sought after and desired," Satrius said. "There are others more desired, who are more silent."

That is, more desired to be gotten rid of.

Those others were Silius and Sabinus.

"Here he comes," Natta said. "Away! Let's leave!"

Satrius and Natta exited the scene just as Sabinus, Arruntius, and Cordus entered the scene.

Seeing Satrius and Natta leaving, Sabinus asked Arruntius and Cordus, "How is it that these beagles haunt the house of Agrippina?"

In Ben Jonson's society, being called a beagle was an insult.

Arruntius said, "Oh, they hunt, they hunt. There is some game here lodged, which they must rouse, to make the great ones sport."

Cordus asked, "Did you observe how they inveighed against Caesar?"

Arruntius said, "Aye, baits, baits for a trap for us to bite at. If I were to have my flesh torn by the public hook, these qualified hangmen should be my company."

The corpses of executed criminals were dragged with a hook — the *uncus* — to the *Gemoniae*, aka Gemonian stairs, a flight of stairs in a corner of the Roman Forum, and displayed for three days. They were then dragged to the Tiber River and either left on the river bank or thrown into the river.

Sejanus wanted his obstacles to be executed and treated in this way.

"Here comes another," Cordus said.

Afer the orator walked by them and then exited.

Arruntius said:

"Aye, there's a man — Afer the orator!

"He is one who has phrases, figures of speech, and metaphorical fine flowers to strew his rhetoric with, and he is in a hurry to get himself a notable reputation or name by any proposal or opportunity where blood or gain are objects. He steeps his words, when he would kill, in artificial tears — he is the crocodile of Tiber!

"Him I love, that man is mine. He has my heart, and voice, when I would curse, he, he!"

Arruntius loved to curse Afer the orator.

"Afer" means "African," and crocodiles come from Africa.

Sabinus said:

"Contemn and heap scorn on the slaves;

"Their present lives will be their future graves."

Sabinus, Arruntius, and Cordus exited.

Silius, Agrippina, Nero, and Sosia talked together.

Sosia was Silius' wife. She was also a friend to Agrippina.

Nero was Agrippina's oldest son. If Drusus Senior, Tiberius' son, were to die, Nero would be expected to become Emperor when Tiberius died.

Silius said to Agrippina, "May it please Your Highness not to forget yourself — I dare not, without detriment to my manners, trouble you farther."

"Farewell, noble Silius," Agrippina said.

"Most royal princess," Silius replied.

"Sosia stays with us?" Agrippina asked.

"She is your servant, and she owes Your Grace an honest but unprofitable love," Silius said.

"How can that be, when there's no gain but virtue's?" Agrippina asked.

Silius replied:

"You take the moral, not the politic sense.

"I meant, as she is bold, and free of speech, earnest to utter what her zealous thought labors with, in honor of your house, which act, as it is simply born in her and done without calculation, partakes of love and honesty, but may, by the over-often and untimely use, turn to your loss and danger — for your state and high rank is waited on by as many envies as there are eyes; and every second guest your tables take is a paid-for spy, to observe who goes, who comes, what conference you have, with whom, where, when, what the discourse is, what the looks, the thoughts of every person there, and they take these things out of context, and make a different substance out of it."

Sosia was honest but outspoken, and her being outspoken was politically dangerous to Agrippina when spies were watching her and her household and were willing to misinterpret words to put Agrippina and her associates in the worst possible light.

Agrippina said:

"Hear me, Silius.

"If all Tiberius' body were stuck with eyes, and every wall and hanging in my house as transparent as this fine linen I wear, or as transparent as air; yea, and if Sejanus had both his ears as long as to reach into my inmost private room,

I would hate to whisper any thought, or change an act, even to be made Juno's rival.

"Virtue's forces show always noblest in conspicuous courses of action."

According to Virgil's *Aeneid*: "Rumor has wings and many feathers. Her many eyes never sleep, and she has many tongues and many ears. By night she flies, and by day she watches and listens. She values lies as much as she values truths."

Juno was the wife of Jupiter, King of the gods, and so she was Queen of the gods. One kind of rival of hers would be someone who wanted to be Queen. Another kind of rival would be someone who wanted to sleep with her husband.

Juno was a jealous wife with an often-adulterous husband, and she hated her sex rivals and often punished them. For example, she punished Io, one of the many mortal women with whom Jupiter slept, by changing her into a cow. One of Juno's servants was Argus Panoptes, who had one hundred eyes, which never slept all at the same time. He was given the job of always keeping an eye on Io, so that she could not be rescued. Jupiter sent Mercury, the swift messenger of the god, to charm Argus asleep and then kill him. After the act was performed, Jupiter changed Io back into a human woman.

Apollo was once challenged to a music contest by a satyr. Midas judged the contest, and he declared that the satyr had won the contest. Angry, Apollo gave Midas donkey ears. Midas kept his long ears hidden; no one knew about them except his barber, who was forbidden to tell anyone Midas' secret. The barber, wanting to tell the secret, dug a hole in the ground, whispered the secret into the hole, and then filled it up again. Reeds grew in that spot, and when wind blew through the reeds, they whispered, "Midas has the ears of an ass." Soon, everyone knew the secret.

Agrippina was a strong woman who did not want to restrict her freedom of speech and of actions in order to be safe.

Silius responded:

"It is great, and bravely spoken, like the spirit of Agrippina; yet Your Highness knows that there is neither loss nor shame in careful foresight.

"Few can do what all should do: Beware enough.

"You may perceive with what officious and eagerly attentive face Satrius and Natta, Afer and the rest, visit your house recently, to inquire the secrets, and with what bold and privileged art they rail against Augusta, yea, and at Tiberius, tell tricks of Livia, and Sejanus, all to excite and call your indignation on, so that they might hear it at more liberty."

The confederates of Sejanus were deliberately speaking in such a way that could get Agrippina overly emotional and cause her to say things that she would not say if she were calm. She could be overly emotional because of anger or because of pride.

In his conversation with Sejanus, Postumus had spoken of an attempt to make Agrippina overly emotional with excessive praise. Sabinus, however, had put a stop to it.

"You're too suspicious, Silius," Agrippina said.

Silius responded:

"I pray to the gods that I am so, Agrippina, but I fear some subtle intrigue.

"They who dared to strike at so example-less — unparalleled — and unblamed a life as that of the renowned Germanicus will not rest content with that exploit alone.

"He who has injured one person, threatens many."

Nero, Agrippina's oldest son, said, "It would be best to rip out their tongues, sear and burn out their eyes, when next they come."

"That is a fit reward for spies," Sosia said.

Drusus Junior, Agrippina's middle son, entered the room and said, "Have you heard the rumor?"

"What rumor?" Agrippina asked.

"Drusus Senior is dying," Drusus Junior said.

Drusus Senior was the son of Tiberius. "Drusus Senior" means "Drusus the Older," and "Drusus Junior" means "Drusus the Younger." After the boys' father, Germanicus, had died, however, Tiberius had given the boys into the care of his — Tiberius' — son: Drusus Senior.

"Dying?" Agrippina said.

"That's strange!" Nero said.

"You were with him last night," Agrippina said.

Drusus Junior said, "Someone met Eudemus the physician who was sent for just now. Eudemus thinks that Drusus Senior cannot live."

Silius said, "Thinks? If he has arrived at that opinion, he *knows*, or no one knows."

"This is quick!" Agrippina said. "What is said to be his disease?"

Silius said quietly to himself, "Poison, poison —"

Hearing him, but not clearly, Agrippina said, "What, Silius!"

"What's that?" Nero asked.

"Nay, nothing," Silius said. "There was, recently, a certain blow given on the face."

"Aye, to Sejanus?" Nero asked.

"True," Silius said.

"And what of that?" Drusus Junior asked.

"I'm glad I'm not the person who gave Sejanus that blow," Silius said.

"But there is something else?" Nero asked.

Silius answered, "Yes, private meetings, with a great lady, at a physician's, and a wife turned away and divorced —"

"Ha!" Nero said.

"Trifles, mere trifles," Silius said.

He was unwilling to clearly state what he believed was the truth.

He then asked, "What wisdom's now in the streets? What's in the common mouth?"

Drusus Junior said, "Fears, whisperings, tumults, noise, I don't know what. They say the Senate is meeting."

"I'll go there, immediately, and see what's in the forge," Silius said. "I'll see what's cooking."

"Good Silius, do," Agrippina said. "Sosia and I will go in."

Silius said:

"Make haste, my lords, to visit the sick prince. Tender your loves and sorrows to the people.

"This Sejanus, trust my divining soul, has plots on all;

"No tree that stops his view but must fall."

In other words, Sejanus was out to get rid of everyone who stood between him and his becoming Emperor.

Everyone exited.

At this point in Ben Jonson's play, a Chorus of Musicians performed.

CHAPTER 3
— 3.1 —

Heralds, Lictors, Varro, Sejanus, Latiaris, Cotta, and Afer entered the Senate.

In meetings of the Senators, the Heralds were criers.

Lictors held the *fasces* — a bundle of rods and an axe that served as a symbol of power — as they preceded magistrates through the streets.

Varro was one of the current Consuls. His father and Silius had been enemies, and Varro was hostile toward Silius. In this society, that animus, aka hostility, was a sign that Varro's motives were honest.

Latiaris was a supporter of Sejanus.

Cotta was a man without scruples.

Sejanus said to Varro:

"It is only you who must make the case against Silius, Varro. Neither I nor Caesar may appear therein, except in your defense, who are the Consul, and under the color — the pretense — of late enmity between your father and his [actually, should be *him* — Silius, not Silius' father], may better do it, as free from all suspicion of a plot and machination."

He handed Varro some notes and then continued:

"Here are your notes, showing you what points to touch on. Read them. Be cunning in them. Afer has them, too."

"But is he — Silius — summoned to come to the Senate for trial?" Varro asked.

"No," Sejanus said. "It was considered by Caesar and concluded as most fitting to take him unprepared."

Afer added, "And prosecute all under the name of treason."

"I understand," Varro said.

Sabinus, Gallus, Lepidus, and Arruntius entered the scene and conferred privately. They were Germanicans.

Gallus was the husband of Vipsania, who had been Tiberius' first wife.

Like Arruntius, Lepidus was a Senator of integrity.

Sabinus said, "His son, Drusus Senior, being dead, Caesar will not be here."

"What should the business of this Senate be?" Gallus asked.

Arruntius said:

"That is something the subtle whisperers can tell you. We, who are the good-dull-noble lookers-on, are called on only to keep the marble benches warm.

"What should we do with those deep mysteries, proper to these fine heads? Let them alone.

"Our ignorance may, perchance, help us be saved from whips and Furies."

Furies, who were often depicted holding a whip of scorpions in one hand and a torch in the other, were avenging spirits from the Land of the Dead. They especially punished those who killed relatives.

"See, see, see, their action and operation!" Gallus said.

The Germanicans watched the followers of Sejanus in action and commented on what they saw. No followers of Sejanus overheard them.

Arruntius said, "Aye, now their heads do travail, now they work. Their faces run like shuttles used in weaving; they are weaving some skillfully intricate cobweb to catch flies."

"Watch," Sabinus said. "They take their places."

"What, so low!" Arruntius said.

The Senators were sitting on lower benches, not in their usual higher benches, as a sign of mourning for the death of Drusus Senior.

"Oh, yes," Gallus said. "They must be seen to flatter Caesar's grief, though but in sitting."

Varro said to the Heralds, "Bid silence for us. Bring the Senate to order."

"Silence!" the First Herald shouted.

Varro said, "Fathers conscript, may this our present meeting turn fair and fortunate to the commonwealth."

"Fathers conscript" are Senators.

Silius and some other Senators entered the scene.

"Look, Silius enters," Sejanus said.

"Hail, grave fathers!" Silius said.

A Lictor said loudly:

"Stand! Stay where you are!

"Silius, forbear thy place. Don't sit among the Senators."

The Senators, surprised, said, "What!"

The First Herald said, "Silius, stand forth. The Consul Varro has to charge thee."

A Lictor shouted, "Make way for Caesar! Make room for Caesar!"

Arruntius said to Sabinus, "Has he come, too? In that case, then, expect a trick."

Sabinus replied, "Silius accused? Surely he will answer nobly."

Tiberius and some attendants entered the scene.

Because his son, Drusus Senior, had just died, Tiberius had not been expected to show up in the Senate. Tiberius was showing that he was made of sterner stuff. He also would say that he expected the Senators not to allow themselves to droop because of the death of Drusus Senior.

Tiberius said:

"We stand amazed, fathers, to behold this general dejection. For what reason sit Rome's Consuls thus weeping, as if they had lost all the remembrance both of style and place?

"It is not becoming."

As a sign of grieving, the Senators were not sitting in their usual places of high honor.

Tiberius continued:

"No woes are of fit weight to make the honor of the Empire stoop —

"Though I, in my private self, may meet just reprehension, that so suddenly, and in so fresh a grief following the death of Drusus Senior, would greet the Senate, when private tongues of kinsmen and allies, inspired with comforts, loathly are endured, the face of men not seen, and scarcely the day, to thousands who communicate our loss."

Tiberius acknowledged that he could be criticized for showing up in the Senate after the death of his son, while thousands of others would communicate and share their grief at the kind of loss he had suffered by loathly enduring seeing other men and hearing their comforting words and by scarcely even enduring the sight of day.

Tiberius continued:

"Nor can I accuse these people of weakness, since they take but natural ways, yet I must seek for stronger aids and draw out those fair helps from warm embraces of the commonwealth — the Roman people.

"Our mother, great Augusta, is old and struck with time, ourself impressed with aged characters — the marks of time.

"Drusus Senior is gone, his children young, and babes."

Drusus Senior had two children who lived to adulthood: Livia Julia and Tiberius Julius Caesar Nero Gemellus, who was co-heir with Caligula. When Tiberius died in 37 C.E., Caligula either had Drusus Senior's son killed or forced him to kill himself.

A meeting of the Senate took place in 23 C.E., after the death of Drusus Senior. The trial of Silius took place in 24 C.E. The trial of Cordus took place in 25 C.E. Ben Jonson conflated these three events into this one event you are reading about now. Such telescoping of time is common in history plays of the time.

Tiberius continued:

"Our aims must now reflect on and consider those who may give timely succor to these present ills and are our only glad-surviving hopes: the noble issue of Germanicus: Nero and Drusus Junior.

"Might it please the Consul to bring them in with honor — they both wait outside this meeting place —

"I would present them to the Senate's care and raise those suns — and sons — of joy, which should drink up these floods of sorrow in your drowned eyes."

Arruntius said to Sabinus, "By Jove, I am not Oedipus enough to understand this Sphinx."

The Sphinx is a mythological creature with the head of a woman and the body of a lion. In Sophocles' tragedy *Oedipus Rex*, the Sphinx asks Oedipus this riddle: What goes on four legs in the morning, two legs at noon, and three legs in the evening? If Oedipus cannot answer this riddle correctly, the Sphinx will kill him. Fortunately, Oedipus does answer the riddle correctly: Man, who goes on hands and knees as a crawling baby, two legs as a healthy adult, and two legs and a cane as an old person.

Sabinus replied, "The princes come."

Nero and Drusus Junior and some attendants entered the scene.

Tiberius said to Nero and Drusus Junior:

"Approach, noble Nero, noble Drusus Junior."

Tiberius then said to the Senators:

"These princes, fathers, when their parent died, I gave to their uncle, with this prayer:

"That, though he'd proper, legitimate, and admirable children of his own, he would bring up and foster these boys no less than he would bring up that self-blood — his own children — and by that act confirm their worths to him and to posterity."

When Germanicus had died, Tiberius had given his — Germanicus' — boys, Nero and Drusus Junior, into the care of their uncle: Drusus Senior. But now Drusus Senior had died.

Drusus Senior and the boys' father, Germanicus, had been step-brothers. Germanicus was the nephew of Tiberius, who adopted him. Tiberius will call Germanicus Augustus' nephew, but Ben Jonson's society used the word "nephew" loosely. Germanicus was Augustus' great-nephew.

Tiberius continued speaking to the Senators:

"Drusus Senior having died and been taken away from here, I turn my prayers to you, Senators, and, before our country and our gods, I beseech you to take, and rule, Augustus' nephew's sons — the sons of Germanicus — sprung of the noblest ancestors; and so accomplish and fulfill both my duty and your own."

Tiberius then said:

"Nero and Drusus Junior, these Senators shall be to you in place of parents, these Senators shall be your fathers, these shall be, and not unfitly; for you are so born as all your good or ill is the commonwealth's."

Tiberius said to the Senators:

"Receive them, you strong guardians."

Tiberius prayed to the gods:

"And, blest gods, make all their actions answer to their bloods.

"Let their great titles find increase by them, and let they not find increase by titles. Set them, as in place and rank, so in example, above all the Romans, and may they know no rivals but themselves.

"Let Fortune give them nothing they don't deserve but attend upon their virtue — and let virtue always come forth greater than hope, and better than their fame."

Tiberius said to the Senators:

"Relieve and support me, fathers, with your general and collective voice."

The Senators answered, "May all the gods consent to Caesar's wish, and add to any honors that may crown the hopeful issue — promising children — of Germanicus!"

Tiberius said, "We thank you, reverend fathers, on their behalf."

Tiberius had said all the right words regarding Germanicus' children.

Arruntius, Sabinus, and Gallus, seated together, whispered among themselves.

Arruntius said, "If this were true now! But the space, the space between the breast and lips — Tiberius' heart lies a thought farther than another man's."

Arruntius believed that there was a difference between Tiberius' private thoughts and his public words.

Tiberius said:

"My comforts are so flowing in my joys as, in them, all my streams of grief are lost, no less than are land waters in the sea, or showers in rivers, although their cause was such as might have sprinkled even the gods with tears.

"Yet since the greater does embrace the less, we covetously — eagerly — obey."

Tiberius was not crying. His comforts — the Senators' support of Nero and Drusus Junior — outweighed his grief. So said Tiberius.

"Well acted, Caesar," Arruntius said.

Tiberius said:

"And now I am the happy witness made of your so-much-desired affections to this great issue, Nero and Drusus Junior, I could wish the Fates would here set a peaceful period — end — to my days.

The three Fates determined the length of mortal lives. Clotho spun the thread of life, Lachesis measured it, and Atropos cut it. When a mortal's thread of life was cut, the mortal died.

Tiberius continued:

"However, to my labors, I entreat, and beg some fit ease of this Senate."

"Laugh, fathers, laugh!" Arruntius said. "Have you no spleens about you?"

In Ben Jonson's time, the spleen was regarded as the source of laughter — and of melancholy.

Tiberius now spoke about his desire or supposed desire to delegate his authority to others and so lessen the burden that rested on his own shoulders:

"The burden is too heavy that I sustain on my unwilling shoulders; and I pray that it may be taken off, and conferred from me to the Consuls, or some other Roman, more able and more worthy than I."

"Laugh on, still," Arruntius said.

"Why, this renders suspect all the rest!" Sabinus said.

"It poisons all," Gallus said.

"Oh, do you taste — perceive — it then?" Arruntius said.

"It takes away my faith in anything that he shall hereafter speak," Sabinus said.

They did not believe that Tiberius wished to delegate authority. Not believing that, they did not believe what Tiberius had said earlier about the care of Germanicus' children — nor would they believe whatever Tiberius would say hereafter.

Arruntius said, "Aye, to pray for that which would be to his head as hot as thunder — against which he wears that charm — should but the court receive him at his word."

According to Suetonius, Tiberius was afraid of thunder and lightning and wore a laurel wreath during lightning storms because of a folk belief that laurel was a protection against lightning.

"Hear!" Gallus shouted.

Gallus wanted everyone to pay attention to and listen to Tiberius.

Tiberius said, "For myself, I know my weakness, and I so little covet — like some others gone past — the weight that will oppress me. My ambition is the counterpoint."

Ambition was the counterpoint — the opposite — to what Tiberius said he really wanted: seclusion.

Rather than power and responsibility, Tiberius was saying that he wanted peace, quiet, and seclusion.

"Finely maintained," Arruntius said. "It is good still."

Sejanus said, "But Rome, whose blood, whose nerves, whose life, whose very frame relies on Caesar's strength, no less than heaven relies on Atlas, cannot admit it except with general ruin."

Atlas held up the sky on his shoulders.

Allowing Tiberius to go into seclusion would ruin Rome. So said Sejanus.

Arruntius said about Sejanus, "Ah! Are you there, to bring him off and aid and rescue him?"

And take his place? And then ruin Rome?

Sejanus said, "Let Caesar no more, then, urge a point so contrary to Caesar's greatness, the grieved Senate's vows, or Rome's necessity."

Sejanus was saying that Tiberius ought not to go into seclusion.

"He comes about," Gallus said.

"More nimbly than Vertumnus," Arruntius said.

Vertumnus was the god of seasons, and of changes.

Tiberius said:

"For the benefit of the public, I may be persuaded to show I can neglect all private aims, although I desire my rest.

"But if the Senate still commands me to serve, I must be glad to practice my obedience."

"You must, and will, sir," Arruntius said. "We do know it."

In other words: You, Tiberius, will continue to be Emperor. All these words that you are speaking now are part of an act.

The Senators shouted:

"Caesar!

"Live long, and happy, great and royal Caesar!

"The gods preserve thee, and thy modesty [your moderation], thy wisdom, and thy innocence!"

"Where is it?" Arruntius said. "The prayer's made before the subject."

Arruntius was saying that the Senators were praying for the preservation of qualities that Tiberius did not have. If he did not have them, how could they be preserved?

The Senators shouted, "Guard his meekness, Jove, his piety, his care, his bounty —"

Arruntius said quietly, "And his tricky subtlety, I'll put in — yet he'll keep that himself, without the help of the gods. All prayers are vain for him."

Tiberius said:

"We will not hold your patience, fathers, with long answer, but shall still contend to be what you desire, and work to satisfy so great a hope.

"Proceed to your affairs."

The trial of Silius was about to begin.

Afer came forward.

"Now, Silius, guard thee," Arruntius said. "The curtain's drawing. Something's about to happen. Afer advances."

The First Herald shouted, "Silence!"

"Cite Caius Silius," Afer said.

"Caius Silius!" the First Herald shouted.

Silius came forward and said, "Here."

Afer began his speech by mentioning a revolt led by Julius Sacrovir of the Aedui in Gaul in 21 C.E., a revolt that Silius, then the governor of upper Germany, had put down with two Roman legions.

Afer said:

"The triumph that thou had in Germany for thy recent victory over Sacrovir, thou have enjoyed so freely, Caius Silius, that no man maliciously envied thee it; nor would Caesar or Rome permit and allow that thou would be then defrauded of any honors that thy deserts could claim in the fair service of the commonwealth.

"But now, if after all their loves and graces, thy actions and their courses being discovered and made known, it shall appear to Caesar, and this Senate, thou have defiled those glories with thy crimes —"

Silius interrupted, " — crimes?"

"Patience, Silius," Afer said.

Silius replied:

"Tell thy mule about patience! I am a Roman.

"What are my crimes? Proclaim them.

"Am I too rich? Too honest for the times? Have I treasure, jewels, land, or houses that some informer gapes for?"

People could bring unjustified charges against someone in the hope that the accused person's property would be seized and the accuser would get a part of it. These people's mouths gape — open wide — with greed.

Silius continued:

"Is my strength too much to be admitted? Or my knowledge?

"These now are crimes."

Afer said, "Silius, if the name of crime makes you so angry and irritates thee, with what impotence — inability to defend yourself, and inability to restrain your passions — will thou endure the matter to be searched?"

Silius replied:

"I tell thee, Afer, with more scorn than fear: Employ your mercenary — hired — tongue and art.

"Where's my accuser?"

Varro came forward and said, "Here."

Arruntius said, "Varro? The Consul? Is he thrust in the plot?"

Varro said:

"It is I who accuse thee, Silius.

"Against the majesty of Rome and Caesar, I do pronounce and declare thee here a guilty cause and guilty agent, first, of beginning and occasioning, and next, of drawing out the war in Gallia, for which thou recently enjoyed a triumph in Germany.

"Thou falsely pretended a long time that Sacrovir was an enemy, only to make thy provisions and revenue for fighting the war from the state more, while thou, and thy wife Sosia, plundered the province.

"Wherein, with sordid-base desire of gain, thou have discredited thy actions' worth and been a traitor to the state."

According to Varro, Silius had done good service in defeating Sacrovir, but he had made the war last longer than it needed to in order to get money from Rome to fight the war. Also, Silius and his wife had plundered Gaul, where the war took place.

"Thou lie," Silius said.

"I thank thee, Silius," Arruntius said quietly. "Speak so still, and often."

Varro said to Tiberius, "If I do not prove my allegations, Caesar, but unjustly have called Silius into trial, here I bind myself to suffer what I claim against him, and yield to have what I have spoken confirmed by judgment of the court, and all good men."

Silius said to Tiberius, "Caesar, I crave to have my case deferred until this man's Consulship is over."

Tiberius said, "We cannot, nor may we grant it."

"Why?" Silius asked. "Shall he appoint my day of trial? Shall he impeach me? Is he my accuser? And must he be my judge?"

Tiberius said:

"It has been usual, and it is a right that *custom* has allowed the magistrate, to call forth private men and to appoint their day.

"This privilege we may not in the Consul see infringed, by whose deep watches and industrious care it is so accomplished with labor and managed that the commonwealth receives no loss by any oblique, evil course."

Silius said, "Caesar, thy fraud is worse than violence."

The fraud was pretending that the Consul Varro had the moral authority to be both the accuser and one of the judges of Silius. Tiberius had just referred to custom, by which he meant extraordinary privileges given to Consuls in times of crisis, but there was now no time of crisis.

Tiberius said:

"Silius, don't mistake us.

"We dare not use the credit and authority of the Consul to thy wrong, but we only preserve and protect his place and power so far as it concerns the dignity and honor of the state."

"Believe him, Silius," Arruntius said.

He was sarcastic.

Overhearing him, Cotta said, "Why, so he may, Arruntius."

"I say so," Arruntius said. "And he may choose to."

He may choose to believe Tiberius. But Arruntius will not choose to believe Tiberius.

Tiberius said, "By the Capitol, and all our gods, except for when the dear Republic, our sacred laws, and just authority are interessed — involved and have an interest in — therein, I should be silent."

Afer said, "May it please Caesar to give permission to hold his — Silius' — trial. He shall have justice."

Silius said, "Nay, I shall have law. Shall I not, Afer? Speak."

"Would you have more?" Afer asked.

Silius replied:

"No, my well-spoken man, I would have no more.

"Nor would I have less as long as I might enjoy it natural — by which I mean uncontrived — and not taught to speak unto your present ends.

"And as long as it is free from thine, his, and all your unkind — unnatural — handling, furious enforcing, most unjust presuming, malicious and manifold applying, foul wresting, and impossible construction and interpretation of the law."

Yes, he wanted law, but he wanted law that was justly applied.

"He raves, he raves," Afer said.

Silius replied, "Thou would not dare to tell me so, if thou didn't have Caesar's permission. I can see whose power condemns me."

"This betrays his spirit," Varro said. "This does enough declare what he is."

"What am I?" Silius said. "Speak."

"An enemy to the state," Varro said.

Silius said, "Because I am an enemy to thee, and such corrupted ministers of the state who here are made a present instrument to gratify it with thine own disgrace."

"This, to the Consul, is most insolent!" Sejanus said. "And impious!"

The Consuls performed religious as well as civic duties, and so Sejanus was saying that criticizing a Consul was impious.

Silius said:

"Aye, take part. Take sides. Reveal yourselves.

"Alas, don't I scent your confederacies, your plots and combinations? Don't I know that minion — that darling — sSejanus hates me, and that all this boast of law, and law, is just a form, a net of Vulcan's making, a complete trap, to take that life by a pretext of justice that you pursue in malice?"

Venus had an affair with Mars, the god of war. The two had fallen in lust although Venus, the goddess of sexual passion, was married to Vulcan, the gifted blacksmith god. Vulcan learned of the affair, so he set a trap for the illicit lovers. He created a fine net that bound tightly, he placed the net above his bed, and then he pretended to leave his mansion to journey abroad. Mars ran to Venus, and together they ran to bed. Mars and Venus lay down in bed together, and then the fine net snared them, locked in lust.

Silius' reference to Vulcan's net, however, is unhappy because Vulcan's net caught a guilty — not innocent — couple.

Silius continued:

"Do I lack brain or nostril — to smell a rat — to persuade me that your ends and purposes are made to what they are, before my answer?

"O you impartial gods, a world of wolves-turned-into-men shall not make me accuse your justice, however they provoke me.

"Have I for this so often engaged myself, stood in the heat and fervor of a fight, when Phoebus the sun-god sooner has forsaken the day than I the battlefield against the blue-eyed Gauls and curly-haired Germans, when our

Roman eagles — legionary standards — have fanned the fire with their laboring wings, and there was no blow dealt that left not death behind it?

"And have I for this so often engaged myself when I have charged, alone, into the troops of curly-haired Sicambrians, routed them, and came off the battlefield not with the backward ensigns of a slave, but forward marks, wounds on my breast, and face, wounds that were intended for thee, O Caesar, and thy Rome?"

Silius' scars were on the front of his body, not on the back. He had gotten his scars while fighting, not while running away.

Because Silius and his troops had remained loyal to Rome during a period of unrest, they had saved Rome and had taken the wounds that would have been Rome's had they had not remained loyal.

Silius boasted about this when he returned to Rome, and his boastfulness may have been a cause of his downfall. His enemies believed or said they believed that Silius' boastfulness made Tiberius look weak.

Silius continued:

"And have I this return? Did I, for this, perform so noble and so brave defeat on Sacrovir?

"O Jove, let it become me to boast about my deeds, when he, whom they concern, shall thus forget them!"

Afer said:

"Silius, Silius, these are the common customs and traits of thy blood and temper, when it is high with wine, as now with rage.

"This well agrees with that intemperate boast thou recently made at Agrippina's table, that when all other of the troops were prone to fall into rebellion, only thine remained in their obedience. Thou boasted that thou were the man who saved the Empire, which would have then been lost, had but thy legions, there, rebelled, or mutinied.

"Thou boasted that thy virtue met and fronted every peril.

"Thou boasted that thou gave to Caesar and to Rome their safety.

"Thou boasted that their name, their strength, their spirit, and their state, and even their being was a donative — a gift — from thee."

"Well worded, and most like an orator," Arruntius said.

"Is this true, Silius?" Tiberius asked.

"Save thy question, Caesar," Silius said. "Thy spy, of infamous reputation, has confirmed it."

Indeed, Afer had spied on Agrippina and her household.

"Excellent Roman!" Arruntius said.

"He does answer stoutly," Sabinus said.

"If this is so, there needs no farther ground for charges against him," Sejanus said.

Varro said, "What can more impeach the royal dignity and state of Caesar than to have pressed upon his attention a benefit that he cannot pay for?"

"In this, all Caesar's fortune is made unequal to the courtesy," Cotta said.

In other words: If Silius' claims are true, then Tiberius would never be able to reward him as he deserves.

"His means are clean destroyed, who should requite," Latiaris said.

"Nothing is great enough for Silius' merit," Gallus said.

Arruntius asked Sabinus, "Is Gallus on that side, too?"

Silius said:

"Come, do not hunt and labor so about for circumstantial evidence to make the man — me — guilty whom you have foredoomed and pre-judged.

"Take shorter ways; I'll fall in with your purposes.

"The words were mine; and more I now will say:

"Since I have done thee that great service, Caesar, thou always have feared me, and, in place of grace, returned me hatred. So soon, all best services, with fearful princes, turn into deep injuries in estimation, when they greater rise than can be repaid. Benefits, with you, are of no longer pleasure than you can with ease recompense them; that transcended once, your studies are not how to thank, but kill.

"It is your nature to have all men slaves to you, but you acknowledging to none. The means that make your greatness must not be mentioned when speaking about your greatness. If it is mentioned, it takes so much away, you think; and that which helped shall soonest perish, if it stand within eyesight and is seen, where it may affront and confront or just upbraid the high."

"Allow him to speak no more," Cotta said.

"Just note his spirit," Varro said.

To Varro, Silius was being arrogant.

"This reveals him in the rest," Afer said. "If he is guilty in this, then he is guilty in all."

"Let him be judged," Latiaris said.

"He has spoken enough to prove that he is Caesar's foe," Sejanus said.

"His thoughts look through his words," Cotta said.

"A censure," Sejanus said. "A judgment."

Silius said:

"Wait, wait, most officious Senate!

"I shall immediately cheat thy fury. Silius has not placed his guards within himself, against Fortune's spite, so weakly but he can escape your grasp.

"You Senators are only hands of Lady Fortune. She herself, when virtue does oppose, must lose her threats.

"All that can happen in human life, the frown of Caesar, proud Sejanus' hatred, base Varro's spleen, and Afer's bloodying tongue, the Senate's servile flattery, and these mustered to kill, I'm fortified against, and can look down upon; they are beneath me.

"It is not life that I stand enamored of, for my end shall make me accuse my fate.

"The coward and the valiant man alike must fall; only the cause, and manner how, distinguishes them, which then are gladdest when they cost us dearest.

"Romans, if any are here in this Senate who would like to know how to mock Tiberius' tyranny, look upon Silius, and so learn how to die."

He stabbed himself.

"Oh, desperate act!" Varro said.

"An honorable hand!" Arruntius said.

"Look and see if he is dead," Tiberius ordered.

"It was nobly struck, and home," Sabinus said.

Arruntius said, "My thought did prompt him to it. He read my mind. Farewell, Silius! Be famous forever for thy great example."

Tiberius said, "We are not pleased in this sad accident that thus has forestalled and abused our mercy. We had intended to preserve thee, noble Roman, and to anticipate thy hopes."

Silius had killed himself so that Tiberius and the Romans could not execute him, but now that Silius was dead, Tiberius was saying that he would have shown mercy to Silius.

Arruntius did not believe Tiberius.

"Excellent wolf!" Arruntius said. "Now that he is full, he howls."

Sejanus said, "Caesar does wrong his own dignity and safety, thus to mourn the deserved end of so professed a traitor, and he does, by this lenience of his, instruct others as factious to the like offence."

"The confiscation merely of his estate would have been enough," Tiberius said.

"Oh, that was gaped for, then?" Arruntius said.

The accusers' mouths had gaped wide open in anticipation of swallowing Silius' estate. When an estate was confiscated, informers received part of it.

"Remove the body," Varro said to the Lictors.

They carried the body out.

"Let a summons go out for Sosia," Sejanus said.

Sosia was the wife of Silius.

"Let her be proscribed," Gallus said. "And for the goods, I think it fitting that half go to the public treasury, half to the children."

Silius and Sosia had children.

When Sosia was proscribed, she would be exiled and lose her estate.

By committing suicide before being proscribed, Silius had avoided proscription.

By law, one quarter of the confiscated wealth would go to the accusers.

Lepidus said:

"With the leave of Caesar, I would think that a fourth part, which the law does cast on the informers, should be enough; the rest go to the children —

"By doing this, the prince — Tiberius — shall show humanity and bounty, not to force them by their want, which in their parents' trespass they deserved, to take ill courses."

"It shall please us," Tiberius said.

Arruntius said:

"Aye, out of necessity.

"This Lepidus is grave and honest, and I have observed a moderation always in all his judgments."

Sabinus said, "And inclining to the better course of action —"

Cordus, guarded by Lictors, Satrius, and Natta, entered the scene.

Arruntius said:

"Wait, who's this?

"Cremutius Cordus? What! Is he brought in? More blood to the banquet?

"Noble Cordus, I wish thee good. Be as thy writings: free, open, candid, and honest."

Arruntius was talking quietly. Cordus did not hear him.

"Who is he?" Tiberius asked.

"He is here because of the annals, Caesar," Sejanus said.

Annals are history books that cover years in chronological order.

"Cremutius Cordus!" the first Herald shouted.

"Here," Cordus said.

"Satrius Secundus, Pinnarius Natta, you are his accusers," the First Herald said.

Arruntius said, "They are two of Sejanus' bloodhounds, whom he breeds with human flesh, to bay at citizens."

Afer said to Satrius and Natta, "Stand forth before the Senate, and confront him."

Satrius said, "I do accuse thee here, Cremutius Cordus, to be a man factious and dangerous, a sower of sedition in the state, a turbulent and discontented spirit, which I will prove from thine own writings here, the annals thou have published, where thou bite the present age, and with a viper's tooth, being a member of it, dare to do that ill which never yet degenerate and unworthy-of-family bastard did upon his parent."

Vipers were said to give birth by the process of the progeny biting their way out of the parent.

Natta said, "To this I subscribe, and, out of a world of more particulars, cite only one instance as proof: Comparing men and times, thou praise Brutus, and affirm that 'Cassius was the last of all the Romans.'"

"What!" Cordus said. "What are we, then?"

The answer, of course, is: We are Romans.

"What is Caesar?" Varro asked. "Nothing?"

Afer said:

"My lords, this strikes at every Roman's private, personal interest, in whom reigns gentry and rank and nobility and grandeur of spirit and mettle, to have a Brutus brought in parallel — a parricide, an enemy of his country — ranked and preferred to any real worth that Rome now holds."

Brutus was a parricide in that he had helped kill the father of his country: Julius Caesar. In Latin Brutus was *patriae parentis parricida*.

Afer continued:

"This is most strangely abusive, vituperative, most full of spite and insolent upbraiding.

"Nor is it the time alone that is here dispraised and held in contempt, but the whole man of time, yea, Caesar's self, brought into disvalue; and he — Caesar — is aimed at most by oblique glance — covert allusion — of his licentious pen.

"Caesar, if Cassius were the last of the Romans, thou have no name, no reputation, no status."

"The whole man of time" is praise of Tiberius: He is "the whole man" produced by the processes of time.

"Let's hear him answer," Tiberius said. "Silence."

Cordus said:

"So innocent I am of any evil deed, my lords, that only the words I have written are argued to be evidence; yet those words do not affect either prince or prince's parent — either Tiberius or his father, Caesar Augustus.

"Your law of treason comprehends and includes only malicious words directly affecting princes to be treason.

"I am charged to have praised Brutus and Cassius, whose deeds, when many more besides myself have written about them, not one has mentioned them without honoring them.

"Great Titus Livius, aka Livy, a Roman historian great for eloquence and authority among us, in his *History*, with so great praises did extol Pompey that often Caesar Augustus called Livy a Pompeian — yet this did not hurt their friendship.

"In his book Livy often names Metellus Scipio, Lucius Afranius, yea, the same Cassius, and this same Brutus, too, as worthiest men; not thieves and parricides, which negative titles and stigma are now imposed upon their reputations."

Metellus Scipio and Lucius Afranius fought against Julius Caesar and were defeated.

Cassius and Brutus assassinated Julius Caesar and then fought against Octavian (later named Caesar Augustus) and were defeated.

Cordus continued:

"Asinius Pollio's writings on the civil war quite throughout give them a noble memory.

"Similarly, Messalla gave a noble memory about and gave renown to his general Cassius — yet both of these men lived with Augustus, full of wealth and honors."

Messalla fought under Cassius and then wrote a history about the civil wars.

Cordus continued:

"To Cicero's book, where Cato was heaved up equal with heaven, what else did Caesar answer, being then dictator, but with a penned oration, as if before the judges?"

Cicero wrote a book titled *Cato*, which praised Cato the Younger, and Julius Caesar wrote an opposing book in response titled *Anticato*.

Cordus continued:

"Do but see Antonius' letters; read but Brutus' pleadings, what vile reproach they hold against Augustus — false, I confess, but with much bitterness.

"The epigrams of Roman authors Bibaculus and Catullus are read, although they are fully stuffed with spite of both the Caesars; yet deified Julius, and no less Augustus, both endured them and regarded them with contempt — I don't know readily enough to speak it, whether it was done with more equanimity or wisdom; for such obloquies, if they are quietly despised, they die suppressed, but if with rage acknowledged, they are confessed."

Julius Caesar and Augustus Caesar ignored some writings that insulted them. They may have done it with equanimity, not caring about the insults. Or they may have done it with wisdom, knowing that acknowledging the insults and being enraged by them can be interpreted as a confession that the insults are true.

Cordus continued:

"The Greeks I slip by, whose license not alone, but also lust did escape unpunished. Or where someone, by chance, took exception, he revenged the words with words — not deeds.

"But in my work, what could be aimed more free from, or farther off from the time's scandal, than to write of those whom death had exempted from grace or hatred?"

Cordus was writing about dead — not living — people.

Cordus continued:

"Did I, with Brutus and with Cassius, armed, and possessed of the Philippi fields, incense the people in the civil cause of the state with dangerous speeches? Or do they, being slain seventy years ago, as by their images — which the conqueror has not defaced — appears, retain that guilty memory with writers?"

Plutarch wrote an anecdote about Caesar Augustus coming across a statue of his enemy, Brutus, in a town. Rather than defacing or tearing down the statue, he ordered it kept in place.

Cordus continued:

"Posterity pays every man his honor, nor shall there lack, though I am condemned, those who will not only well approve Cassius, and be mindful of great Brutus' honor, but who will, also, make mention of me."

"Freely and nobly spoken," Arruntius said.

"With good temper," Sabinus said. "I like him because he is not moved with passion and strong emotion."

Tiberius and his followers conferred privately.

The Germanicans talked quietly among themselves.

Arruntius said, "Cordus puts them to their whisper."

Speaking out loud, Tiberius said, "Take him away from here. We shall make a decision about him at the next sitting of the Senate."

A Lictor exited with Cordus in his custody.

Ben Jonson does not write about this, but Cordus committed suicide by starving himself.

"In the meantime, order the Aediles to burn his books," Cotta said.

"You have well advised," Sejanus said.

"It is not fitting that such licentious things should live to upbraid the age," Afer said.

"If the age were good, they might," Arruntius said.

The writings might continue to live, at least for a while, as in fact they did. Some copies of his writings were hidden, and they later circulated.

"Let them be burnt," Latiaris said.

"All sought, and burnt, today," Gallus said.

"The court is over," the First Herald said. "Lictors, resume the fasces."

The Lictors carried the fasces as they led the magistrates away.

Everyone except Arruntius, Sabinus, and Lepidus exited.

Lepidus was a Senator of integrity and capability.

"Let them be burnt!" Arruntius said. "Oh, how ridiculous appears the Senate's brainless diligence, whose members think they can, with present power, extinguish the memory of all succeeding times!"

Sabinus said:

"It is true that the book burners look ridiculous, when, contrary to their intention, the punishment of genius makes the authority of the genius increase.

"Nor do they anything, who practice this cruelty of interdiction and prohibition, and this rage of burning, but purchase to themselves rebuke and shame, and to the writers an eternal name."

Lepidus said, "It is an argument that the times are sore and distressed when virtue cannot safely be advanced and promoted, nor vice reproved."

Arruntius replied, "Aye, noble Lepidus. Augustus well foresaw what we should suffer under Tiberius, when he pronounced the Roman race most wretched that should live between so slow jaws, and so long a-bruising."

Suetonius, in his "Life of Tiberius" in *Lives of the Twelve Caesars* (III.21), wrote, in Alexander Thomson's translation, "I know, it is generally believed, that upon Tiberius's quitting the room, after their private conference, those who were in waiting overheard Augustus say, 'Ah! unhappy Roman people, to be ground by the jaws of such a slow devourer!'"

The devouring caused the bruising.

They exited.

<h1 style="text-align:center">— 3.2 —</h1>

Tiberius and Sejanus talked together.

Tiberius said:

"This business has succeeded well, Sejanus — and quite removed all jealousy of practice — all suspicion of a conspiracy — of us against Agrippina and our nephews.

"Now we must think how to plant our traps for the other pair: Sabinus and Arruntius.

"And Gallus, too — however much he flatters us, we know his heart."

Sejanus said:

"Give it some respite, Caesar."

He may have meant for Tiberius to spare Gallus for a while. Or he may have meant to be slow in bringing down the next enemy. Too many enemies being removed too quickly can cause suspicion. Best to let things rest for a while and then go into action again.

Sejanus continued:

"Time shall mature and bring to perfect crown — bring to perfection what we with so good vultures have begun."

At the founding of Rome, vultures appeared to its founders: Romulus and Remus. Tiberius and Sejanus are perhaps attempting to found a new kind of Rome.

Vultures are birds of omen. Good vultures can perhaps mean that good omens predict that the snares Tiberius and Sejanus will set will be successful.

Sejanus continued:

"Sabinus shall be next."

Tiberius objected: "Rather Arruntius."

Sejanus said, "By any means preserve him. His frank tongue, being lent the reins, will take away all thought of malice in your course against the rest. We must keep him to stalk with."

A stalking horse is a horse behind which hunters hide. Sejanus wanted to use Arruntius as a screen behind which he and Tiberius could hunt their prey. Arruntius' tongue would divert attention to himself while Tiberius and Sejanus secretly set their snares.

Tiberius replied, "Dearest head — dearest person — I yield to thy most auspicious plan."

Sejanus said:

"Sir — I've been so long trained up in grace and favor, first with your father, great Augustus, and since then with your most happy bounties so familiar, that I would not sooner commit my hopes or wishes to the gods than to your ears.

"Nor have I ever yet been covetous of overbright and dazzling honors; instead, I have been covetous to watch and work hard for great Caesar's safety, like the most common soldier."

"I concede that what you say is true," Tiberius said.

Sejanus said:

"The only gain, and which I count most fair of all my fortunes, is that mighty Caesar has thought me worthy his alliance.

"Hence begin my hopes."

Tiberius said, "Hmm?"

In other words: What are you getting at, Sejanus?

Sejanus said:

"I have heard that Augustus, in the bestowing of his daughter in marriage, thought without prejudice of equestrian gentlemen of Rome."

Sejanus meant that Caesar Augustus had thought that members of the noble class *and* members of the equestrian class were worthy of marrying his daughter.

Caesar Augustus' daughter was Julia. Her first husband was Marcus Claudius Marcellus, a nephew of Augustus. Marcellus was not born a noble. He died when she was sixteen, and she then married Tiberius and became his second wife.

Sejanus was a member of the equestrian class of citizens, which were ranked just below the noble class. Marriages could be arranged between the children of the two social classes to strengthen alliances. Sejanus' daughter had been betrothed to a son of the future emperor Claudius, who was a nephew of Tiberius, but a few days after the betrothal, Claudius' son died, according to Suetonius, by choking to death on a pear he had thrown into the air and caught in his mouth.

Sejanus continued:

"If this is so — I don't know how to hope for so great a favor — but if a husband should be sought for Livia, and I should be had in mind, as Caesar's friend, I would but properly use the glory of the familial relationship."

Livia was the widow of Drusus Senior and the sister of Germanicus. A marriage to her would be a politically wise move for Sejanus. Germanicus had two younger siblings: Livia and Claudius, the future Roman Emperor.

Sejanus continued:

"It should not make me slothful, or less caring about Caesar's state; it would be enough to me if it did confirm, establish, and strengthen my weak house — family — against the now unequal opposition of Agrippina; and for dear regard to my children, this I wish.

"I myself have no ambition farther than to end my days in service of so dear a master."

Tiberius replied:

"We cannot but commend thy piety — filial duty and grateful devotion — most loved Sejanus, in acknowledging those bounties, which we, faintly, remember.

"But to thy suit.

"The rest of mortal men, in all their designs and counsels, pursue profit. Princes, alone, are of a different destiny, directing their main actions always to fame and reputation.

"We therefore will take time to think, and answer.

"As for Livia, she can best, herself, decide if she will marry after Drusus, or continue to live in the family as a widow; besides, she has a mother, and a grandam yet, whose nearer counsels she may guide herself by —

"But I will simply deal with this matter straightforwardly."

Livia's grandmother was Augusta (Tiberius' mother), and Livia's mother was Antonia the Younger, the daughter of Marc Antony and Octavia.

Tiberius continued:

"That enmity that thou fear in Agrippina would burn more if Livia's marriage should, as it would, divide in parts the imperial house.

"A rivalry between the women might break forth, and discord might ruin the sons and nephews on both hands.

"What if it causes some immediate quarreling?

"Thou are not safe, Sejanus, if thou attempt and try and test it. Can thou believe that Livia, first the wife to Caius Caesar, then to my Drusus, now will be contented to grow old with thee, who was born not noble but only a private gentleman of Rome, and raise thee with her — Livia's — loss, if not her shame?"

Livia had been married to Caius Caesar, Augustus' grandson and his possible successor. After his death, she then had been married to Drusus Senior, Tiberius' son and his possible successor.

Tiberius continued:

"Or say that I should wish it, can thou think that the Senate, or the people, who have seen her brother Germanicus, her father, and our ancestors in the highest place of empire, will endure it?

"The state and high office thou hold already is talked about.

"Men murmur at thy greatness; and the nobles do not hesitate, in public, to upbraid thy climbing above our father's — Augustus' — favors, or above thy own degree — and these nobles dare accuse me because of their hate to thee.

"Be wise, dear friend.

"We would not hide these things out of friendship's dear respect.

"Nor will we stand adverse to thine or Livia's designments.

"What we had purposed to thee, in our thought, and with what near degrees of love to bind thee and make thee equal to us, for the present we will forbear to — we will not — speak.

"Only believe thus much, our loved Sejanus: We do not know that height in blood, or honor, which thy virtue, and thy favorable mind toward us, may not aspire to with merit.

"And this we'll proclaim, on all suitable and watched-for public occasions that the Senate or the people shall present to us."

Sejanus replied:

"I am restored, and I have regained my sense, which I had lost in this so blinding suit. Caesar has taught me better to refuse than I knew how to ask."

Sejanus was saying that he had been blinded when making his request to marry Livia, but Tiberius' words had restored his sight — and his sense.

Sejanus realized that Tiberius did not want to be closely related to him.

Sejanus changed the subject:

"How does it please Caesar to embrace my recent advice for leaving Rome?"

"We are resolved to do so," Tiberius said.

Giving him a piece of paper, Sejanus said, "Here are some more motives, which I have thought on since, that may more confirm your decision."

The motives were reasons for leaving Rome.

Tiberius said:

"Careful and solicitous Sejanus!

"We will immediately peruse them.

"Go forward in our main design and prosper."

The main design was the plot to get rid of Sabinus.

Tiberius exited, leaving Sejanus alone.

Sejanus said to himself:

"If those but take — that is, if the motives motivate — I shall prosper, indeed. Dull, heavy Caesar!

"Would thou tell me that thy favors were made crimes — that thy favors to me have been characterized as crime?

"And would thou tell me that my fortunes were esteemed as thy faults for favoring me?

"And would thou tell me that thou, because of me, were hated?

"And would thou not think I would with winged haste anticipate and prevent that change, when thou might win all to thyself again by the sacrifice of me?

"Did those foolish words fly swifter from thy lips than this my brain, this sparkling forge, created me an armor to encounter chance, and thee?

"Well, read my charms — my motives for you to leave Rome — and may they lay that hold upon thy senses as if thou had snuffed up powder of poison hemlock, or drunk the narcotic juice of poppy and of mandrakes.

"Sleep, voluptuous Caesar, and let complacency and carelessness seize on thy stupefied powers, and leave them dead to public cares, awake only to thy lusts — the strength of which makes thy libidinous soul itch to leave Rome; and I have thrust it on, with blaming of the city business, the multitude of suits to thee, the confluence of suitors, and then their importunacies in asking for favors — the manifold distractions he must suffer, besides ill rumors, envies, and reproaches.

"A quiet and retired life, larded and garnished with ease and pleasure, would avoid all of these things.

"And yet, for any weighty and great affair, it — Rome — would be the fittest place to give the soundest counsels.

"By means of this, I shall remove him both from thought and knowledge of his own dearest, most important affairs. I will draw all dispatches through my private hands, and I will know his designments."

Sejanus was the Prefect of the Praetorian Guard, and since the dispatches Sejanus mentioned were carried on horseback by members of the Praetorian Guard, Sejanus could intercept all these important communications and intimately learn their contents.

If Tiberius were away from Rome, he would not intimately know the political affairs going on in Rome.

Sejanus continued:

"And I shall pursue my own designments, make my own strengths, by giving suits and places, conferring dignities and offices on people who will follow me. And these who hate me now, lacking access to him, Tiberius, will make their envy none, or less. For when they see me arbiter of all, they must treat me with honor — or else, with Caesar, fall."

Sejanus exited.

Alone, Tiberius said to himself:

"To marry Livia? Will no less, Sejanus, content thy aims? No lower object?

"Well! Thou know how thou are wrought into our trust, woven in our design; and thou think we must now use thee, whatsoever thy projects are.

"It is true. But yet with caution, and fit care.

"And, now we better think —

He called for a servant:

"Who's there, within?"

A servant entered the room.

"Caesar?" the servant asked.

Still thinking, Tiberius said:

"To leave our journey off would be to sin against our decreed delights, and it would appear to be doubt — or, what still less becomes a prince, low fear.

"Yet, doubt has its own law, and fears have their excuse, where princes' states plead necessary use and vital benefit, as ours does now — more because of Sejanus' pride than all fierce Agrippina's hates beside.

"Those are the dreadful, to-be-feared enemies we raise with favors and make dangerous with praise.

"Those injured by us may have the same desire to harm us, but it is the favorite who has the power to strike us."

The people a highly placed man like Tiberius either rewards or punishes may both want to harm him, but the people whom Tiberius rewards are those who can get close to Tiberius and have the opportunity to harm him.

Tiberius continued:

"And fury ever boils more high and strong,

"Heated with ambition, than revenge of wrong.

"It is then a part of supreme skill to grace

"No man too much, but hold a certain space

"Between the ascender's rise and thine own level, lest, when all the rungs of the ladder are reached, his aim be that: to strike us.

"It is thought —"

Realizing that a servant was in the room, Tiberius said to him, "Is Macro in the palace? Find out. If he is not, go seek him and tell him to come to us."

The servant exited to carry out the errand.

Tiberius said to himself:

"Macro must be the organ we must work by now, though no one is less apt for trust."

Macro was a bad man. Tiberius wanted to pit him against another bad man: Sejanus.

Tiberius continued:

"Need does allow what choice would not. I've heard that the poisonous herb aconite, being timely taken, has a healing might against the scorpion's stroke. We'll give that idea a trial — so that, while two poisons wrestle, we may live.

"Sejanus has a spirit too energetic to be used except to the encounter of his like. We must fight his evil with another evil.

"Excused are wiser sovereigns then, who raise one ill

"Against another, and both safely kill.

"The prince who feeds great natures, they will sway him.

"He who nourishes a lion must obey him."

The servant returned with Macro.

"Macro, we sent for you," Tiberius said.

"I heard so, Caesar," Macro replied.

Tiberius said to the servant, "Leave us for a while."

The servant exited.

Tiberius said, "When you shall know, good Macro, the causes of our sending to you, and the ends, you then will listen more closely — and be pleased that you stand so high, both in our choice and trust."

Macro said, "The humblest place in Caesar's choice or trust may make glad Macro proud, without ambition — except to do Caesar service."

Tiberius said:

"Put aside your courting of us. Let's talk straightforwardly.

"We intend, Macro, to depart the city for a time, and see Campania — not for our pleasures, but to dedicate a pair of temples, one to Jupiter at Capua, the other at Nola, to Augustus. In this great work, perhaps, our stay will be extended beyond our will.

"Now, since we are not ignorant what danger may be born out of even our very shortest absence in a state so subject to envy, and embroiled with hate and faction, we have thought on thee, among a field — a large number — of Romans, worthiest Macro, to be our eye and ear, and to keep a strict watch on Agrippina, Nero, Drusus Junior — aye, and on Sejanus.

"Not that we distrust his loyalty, or that we repent one grace and favor of all that heap we have conferred on him — for that would be to disparage our election of him and call that judgment now in doubt which then seemed as unquestioned as an oracle of a god — but greatness has its cankers and sores.

"Worms and moths breed out of too fit matter in the things that they afterward consume, transferring quite the substance of their makers into themselves."

In other words, Sejanus is ambitious and wants to replace Tiberius as Emperor.

Tiberius continued:

"Macro is sharp and understands. Besides, I know him to be subtle, close, wise, and well-read in man and his large nature. He has studied affections, feelings, and passions, and he knows their springs, their ends, and which way and whether they will work.

"It is proof enough of his great merit that we trust him.

"Then let us get to the point — because our conference cannot be long without suspicion."

People keep a close eye on Emperors, and if they knew that Tiberius and Macro had had a long conversation, they would wonder what they had talked about.

Tiberius continued:

"Here, Macro, we assign thee, both to spy, inform, and chastise. Think, and use thy means, thy ministers, what, where, on whom thou will. Explore, plot, practice underhanded schemes.

"All that thou do in this shall be as if the Senate or the laws had given it privilege, and thou thence styled and given the title of the Savior both of Caesar and of Rome.

"We will not take thy answer except in act — whereto, as thou proceed, we hope to hear by trusted messengers sent from thee to us.

"If it be inquired why we called you, say that you have been given the responsibility to see that our chariots and our horses are ready.

"Be always our loved and — shortly — honored Macro."

Tiberius exited.

Alone, Macro said to himself:

"I will not ask why Caesar bids me to do this, but I will take joy in the fact that he bids me to do this. It is the bliss of courts to be employed, no matter how.

"A prince's power makes all his actions virtue. We, whom he works by, are dumb instruments, to do, but not inquire about why we do something; Tiberius' great purposes are to be served, not searched into and questioned.

"Yet, as that bow is most in hand and used whose owner best knows how to effect, obtain, and accomplish his aims, so let that statesman hope to be of most use and most price, that statesman who can hit his prince's target and scope.

"Nor must he look at what or whom to strike but let loose and shoot our metaphorical arrows at everyone; each mark and target must be alike.

"If the mark were to plot against the fame, the life of one with whom I am like a twin; remove a wife from my warm side, a wife as loved as is the air; do away with each parent; draw my heir in the compass of my plots, though I have only one heir; work all my kin to swift perdition; leave no trap unset, for friendship or for innocence; nay, make the gods all guilty, I would undertake this, which is being imposed on me, both with gain and ease.

"The way to rise is to obey and please.

"He who will thrive in state must neglect the trodden paths that truth and right respect, and trod and try new, wilder ways."

Macro then said something that sounds much like Nietzsche's concept of master morality versus slave morality. In doing so, Macro used "in state" to mean "in high government."

"Virtue, there — in state — is not that narrow thing that she is elsewhere."

In other words: Virtue has a different meaning in state — in high government — than it has elsewhere.

Macro continued:

"Men's fortune there — in state — is virtue; reason there — in state — is their will."

In other words: In high government, virtue is whatever will bring oneself good fortune. And whatever one wills — whatever one desires — is their rational reason for acting.

Macro continued:

"Their license there — in state — is their law; and their observance [deferential service to a superior], there — in state — is their skill [ability to accomplish something]."

In other words: In high government, one's law is their license: One does whatever one wants. And one's ability to accomplish something rests in their deferential service to a superior.

Macro continued:

"Occasion there — in state — is their foil; conscience there — in state — is their stain."

In other words: In high government, opportunity and opportunism are one's attractive adornment. And one's conscience is their disgrace. (Of course, in high government, conscience is to be avoided.)

Macro continued:

"Profit there — in state — is their luster; and whatever else there is, is there — in state — their vain."

In other words: In high government, profit gives oneself luster. And anything other than profit has no value.

In summary: The man who wants to rise in high government must have the morality of a master: What is right is what will benefit himself. This is a reversal of conventional morality — what Nietzsche would call slave morality.

Macro continued:

"If then it is the lust and pleasure of Caesar's power to have raised Sejanus up, and in an hour to overturn him, tumbling him down from the height of all, we are Caesar's ready instrument; and Sejanus' fall may be our rise.

"It is no uncouth, aka unfamiliar, thing

"To see fresh buildings from old ruins spring."

Macro exited.

At this point in Ben Jonson's play, a Chorus of Musicians performed.

CHAPTER 4
— 4.1 —

Gallus and Agrippina talked together in Agrippina's house.

Gallus was the husband of Vipsania, who had been Tiberius' first wife.

Agrippina was upset because Tiberius and Sejanus had attacked friends of hers.

"You must have patience, royal Agrippina," Gallus said.

Agrippina replied:

"I must have vengeance first — and that would be nectar to my famished spirits."

Nectar is the drink of the gods.

Agrippina continued:

"O my Fortune, let what thou prepares against me be sudden! Strike all my powers of understanding blind and let me be ignorant of my destiny to come!

"Let me not fear, I who cannot hope."

Gallus said, "Dear princess, these tyrannies you place on yourself are worse than Caesar's."

Agrippina said:

"Is this the happiness of being born great?

"Always to be aimed at by my enemies? Always to be suspected? To live the subject of all jealousies? To be at least the color — the pretext — made, if not the ground — the cause and reason — to every painted — to every made-up — danger?

"Who would not choose at once to fall, rather than thus to hang forever?"

Gallus began, "You might be safe, if you would —"

Agrippina interrupted:

"— if I would what, my Gallus?

"Be lewd Sejanus' strumpet? Or the bawd to Caesar's lusts now that he has gone to practice lust?"

One well-believed reason for Tiberius' leaving Rome was to find a place where he could indulge his lusts.

Agrippina continued:

"Not even doing these things would make me safe, here where nothing is safe.

"You yourself, while thus you stand but by me, are not safe.

"Was Silius safe? Or the good Sosia safe? Or was my niece, dear Claudia Pulchra, safe? Or innocent Furnius?

"They who very recently have, by being made guilty, added reputation to Afer's eloquence?"

Silius, Sosia, Claudia Pulchra, and Furnius were all found guilty, and their being found guilty advanced the reputation of Afer the orator, who spoke against them.

Claudia Pulchra died in exile in 26 C.E.

Furnius was put to death in in 26 C.E. after being found guilty of committing adultery with Claudia Pulchra.

Agrippina continued:

"O foolish friends, could not such fresh examples warn your loves, but you must buy my favors with that loss to yourselves — and when you might perceive that Caesar's cause of raging must forsake him before his will?"

In other words: Tiberius will cease his raging only when the objects of his rage — his perceived enemies — have been found guilty and disposed of.

Agrippina continued:

"Go away, good Gallus, leave me.

"Here it is dangerous to be seen; to speak is treason; to pay me the least duty is called faction.

"You are unhappy in me, and I am unhappy in everything.

"Where are my sons, Nero and Drusus Junior? We are those who are shot at. Let us fall alone, away from others, and not, in our ruins, sepulcher our friends.

"Or shall we do some action, like the offence they charge us with, to mock their efforts that would make us seem to be guilty by actually becoming guilty? Shall we frustrate practice by anticipating it?

"The danger's equal, whether we are innocent or guilty, for whatever they can contrive, they will make good. No innocence is safe when power contests and challenges that innocence. Nor can they trespass more greatly, whose very being was all crime before."

Nero, Drusus Junior, and Caligula entered the scene.

"Have you heard that Sejanus has come back from Caesar?" Nero asked.

"No. How has he come back? Disgraced?" Gallus asked.

"He is now more graced by Tiberius than ever," Drusus Junior said.

"By what mischance?" Gallus asked

"By a chance occurrence that seemed likely enough at one time to be bad," Caligula said.

"But turned too good, to both," Drusus Junior said.

"What chance occurrence was it?" Gallus asked.

Nero said:

"While Tiberius was sitting at his meal in a farmhouse they call Spelunca, sited by the seaside, among the Fundane Hills, within a natural cave, part of the grotto about the entry fell and overwhelmed some of the waiters; others ran away.

"Only Sejanus, with his knees, hands, face, overhanging Caesar, did oppose himself to the remaining ruins, and was found in that so laboring posture by the soldiers who came to help him.

"With which adventure he has so fixed himself in Caesar's trust that thunder cannot move him, and he has come, with all the height of Caesar's praise, to Rome."

Part of a cave ceiling had fallen, and Sejanus had protected Tiberius by standing over him.

Agrippina said:

"And he has come with the power to turn all those ruins on us and bury whole posterities beneath them.

"Nero, and Drusus Junior, and Caligula, your places are the next in line to succeed Tiberius, and therefore you are most resented by them."

"Them" were Tiberius and Sejanus.

Agrippina continued:

"Think on your birth and blood, awake your spirits, encounter their violence; it is princely when a tyrant does oppose you, and it is a fortune sent to exercise your virtue, as the wind does try and test strong trees, which by vexation grow more sound and firm."

Trees that are buffeted by wind are forced to grow strong roots to survive.

Agrippina continued:

"After your father's fall, and your uncle's fate — the deaths of Germanicus and Drusus Senior — what can you hope for but all the change of stroke and variety of blows and attacks that force or sleight can give?

"So then stand upright; and although you do not act, yet suffer nobly.

"Be worthy of my womb, and take strong cheer.

"What we do know will come, we should not fear."

They exited.

— 4.2 —

Macro, alone, considered his situation.

Tiberius had made it clear to him that he wanted Sejanus watched and gotten rid of, but now Macro was hearing news that Sejanus was again favored by Tiberius. What should Macro do? What would keep him safe? Was Sejanus really reconciled to Tiberius?

Alone, Macro said to himself:

"Has Sejanus returned so soon? And he is renewed in trust and grace!

"Is Caesar then so weak? Or has the place but wrought this alteration with the air, and Caesar, on the next part of his journey, will all repair and make things as they were before?

"Macro, thou are engaged, committed, and involved; and what before was public, now must be thy private, more than before.

"The weal of Caesar fitness did imply, but thine own fate confers necessity on thy employment; and the thoughts borne nearest unto ourselves move swiftest still, and dearest.

"If Sejanus recovers Tiberius' favor, thou are lost: Yea, all the weight of preparation for Sejanus' fall will turn on thee and crush thee.

"Therefore, strike before Sejanus settles, to prevent the like strike against thyself.

"He who knows his advantage is he who presses it home and gives the foremost blow."

He exited.

Latiaris, Rufus, and Opsius talked together.

They were Senators who supported Sejanus, and they were enemies to Sabinus, although Sabinus trusted Latiaris.

Latiaris said:

"It is a service great Sejanus will see well requited and will accept nobly.

"Here place yourselves, at a height between the roof and the ceiling, and when I bring him — Sabinus — to utter words of danger that can be used against him, reveal yourselves and take him."

In his *Annals* IV.69, translated by Alfred John Church and William Jackson Brodribb, Tacitus wrote, "Three senators thrust themselves into the space between the roof and ceiling, a hiding-place as shameful as the treachery was execrable."

In real life, this would be an attic. In theatrical practice, this would be the upper stage, which is between the roof and the upper-stage floor that forms a ceiling for part of the lower stage.

"Has he come?" Rufus asked.

"I'll now go fetch him," Latiaris said.

He exited.

"With good speed," Opsius said. "I long to merit from the state in such an action."

"I hope it will obtain the Consulship for one of us," Rufus said.

"We cannot think of less as a reward to bring in one as dangerous as Sabinus," Opsius said.

Rufus said:

"He was a follower of Germanicus, and he still pays dutiful attention and is a client to Germanicus' wife — the widow Agrippina — and children, though they have declined in favor.

"He is a daily visitant, keeps them company in private and in public, and is noted to be the only client of the house.

"Pray Jove that Sabinus will be free and frank of speech to Latiaris!"

"He's allied to him and trusts him well," Opsius said.

"And he'll return his trust?" Rufus asked.

Opsius answered, "To do an office so welcome to the state, I know no man but would strain nearer bands than kindred —"

According to Opsius, Latiaris and Sabinus were kindred, but that would not stop Latiaris from betraying Sabinus in order to do Tiberius and Sejanus a favor.

"Listen, I hear them coming," Rufus said.

"Let's shift to our hiding holes with silence," Opsius said.

They hid.

Latiaris and Sabinus entered the scene.

Latiaris said:

"It is a noble constancy you show to this afflicted house.

"Unlike the others — the friends of season, aka fair weather friends — you do not follow Fortune. And unlike the others, you do not in the winter of their fate forsake the place whose glories warmed you.

"You are just, and worthy of such a princely patron's love as was the world's renowned Germanicus.

"When I remember his ample merit and see his wife and children made objects of so much envy, jealousy, and hate, it makes me ready to accuse the gods of negligence, as men of tyranny."

Sabinus said, "Germanicus' wife and sons must be patient; so must we."

Latiaris said:

"O Jove! What will become of us, or of the times, when to be high, or noble, are made crimes?

"When having land and treasure are most dangerous faults?"

Having land and treasure can be dangerous; evil men may accuse you of treason in hopes of getting that land and treasure even if it causes the real owner's death.

Sabinus replied:

"When our table, even our bed, assaults our peace and safety?"

During evil times, guests at the table, and spouses in bed, can be spies and informers. Some of Agrippina's guests at the table were spies and informers. Her son Nero's wife told her mother about him, and Nero's wife's mother told Sejanus.

Nero's wife's mother was Livia, who had been seduced by Sejanus.

Sabinus continued:

"When our writings are, by any ill-willed agents who dare apply them to the guilty, made to speak what Tiberius and Sejanus will have, to fit their tyrannous revenge and vengeance?

"When ignorance is scarcely innocence, and knowledge is made a capital offence?

"When not so much but the bare empty shade of liberty is taken away from us by force?

"And when we are made the prey to greedy vultures and vile spies who first transfix us with their murdering eyes?"

In fact, Latiaris, Opsius, and Rufus were right now transfixing Sabinus with their murdering eyes.

Latiaris said:

"I think the genius of the Roman race should not be so extinct but that bright flame of liberty might be revived again, which no good man except with his life should lose, and we should not sit like spent and patient fools, still puffing in the dark at one poor ember, held on by hope, until the last spark is out."

A person should lose his liberty only at the same time he loses his life.

Latiaris said:

"The cause is public, and the honor, the reputation, the immortality of every soul who is not a bastard or a slave in Rome is therein concerned.

"Whereto, if men would change the wearied arm, and, for the weighty shield so long sustained, employ the ready sword, we might have some assurance of our vows, desires, and prayers.

"This ass' fortitude — Sejanus' persistence — does tire us all.

"Active valor must redeem our loss, for nothing else will. The rock and our hard steel — our swords — should meet, to enforce those glorious fires again whose splendor cheered the world, and heat gave life no less than does the sun's."

The image was flint hitting steel and creating sparks to light tinder and start a fire.

Sabinus said:

"It would be better to stay in lasting darkness, and despair of day.

"No ill should force the subject to undertake revolution against the sovereign, any more than hell should make the gods do wrong.

"A good man should and must sit down with loss rather than rise unjustly in rebellion — although when the Romans first did yield themselves to one man's power, they did not mean their lives, their fortunes, and their liberties should be his absolute spoil, as if purchased by the sword."

Latiaris said:

"Why, we are worse, if to be slaves and bondsmen to Caesar's slave — the proud Sejanus — is to be worse!

"He who is all, does all — Sejanus gives Caesar leave to hide his ulcerous and covered-with-ointment face, with his bald crown, at Rhodes, while he here stalks upon the heads of Romans and their princes, free to absolutely rule an empire."

Oops! Ben Jonson made a historical error here. Tiberius was at Rhodes years before this time; he was at Rhodes during part of the reign of his adoptive father: Caesar Augustus. Tiberius was not at Rhodes at the time of this play.

Sabinus said, "Now you touch a point, indeed, wherein he shows his art as well as his power."

"And villainy in both," Latiaris said. "Do you observe where Livia lodges? How Drusus Senior came to be dead? What men have been cut off?"

Sabinus said:

"Yes, those are things distant in time.

"I nearer looked into Sejanus' later practice, where he stands declared a master in his profession.

"First, before Tiberius went, Sejanus wrought his fear and made him think that Agrippina sought his death.

"Then he put those fears in her; he sent her often word, under the show of friendship, to beware of Caesar, for Caesar had laid plots to poison her.

"Sejanus drove them — Tiberius and Agrippina — to frowns, to mutual suspicions, which now in visible hatred have burst out."

Because of Sejanus' machinations, Tiberius and Agrippina each feared that the other was trying to poison him or her.

Sabinus continued:

"Since then, Sejanus has had his hired agents work on Nero, and heave him up and exalt him and feed his pride and his ambition.

"They tell him that Caesar's old.

"They tell him that all the people, yea, all the army have their eyes on him — Nero.

"They tell him that both the people and the army long to have him undertake something of worth, to give the world a hope.

"Through his hired agents, Sejanus bids Nero to court the grace of both the people and the army.

"The easy youth perhaps gives ear, and immediately Sejanus writes this comment about Nero to Caesar:

"'See yonder dangerous boy. Note but the practice of the mother, there. She's linking him, for purposes soon to be revealed, with men of the sword.'

"Here's Caesar put in fright against son and mother — against Nero and Agrippina.

"Yet Sejanus does not stop at this.

"The second brother, Drusus Junior, has a fierce nature and is fitter for Sejanus' snare because Drusus Junior is ambitious and full of malicious envy.

"Sejanus clasps and hugs him, poisons him with praise, tells him what hearts Drusus Junior wears — that is, who is devoted and loyal to him — how bright he stands in popular expectation, that Rome suffers with him in the wrong his mother does him by preferring and promoting Nero.

"Thus Sejanus sets Nero and Drusus Junior asunder, each against the other, devises the course of action that enables him to condemn the two brothers, and he keeps the reputation of being a friend to all, while driving all on to ruin."

Latiaris asked, "Caesar sleeps, and nods at this?"

Sabinus said, "I wish that he might always sleep, bogged in his filthy lusts!"

Opsius and Rufus revealed themselves.

"Treason to Caesar!" Opsius shouted.

"Lay hands upon the traitor, Latiaris, or take the name of traitor thyself," Rufus said.

"I am for Caesar," Latiaris said. "I am on Caesar's side, not on the side of traitors."

They apprehended Sabinus.

"Am I then caught?" Sabinus said.

"What do you think, sir?" Rufus said. "You are."

Sabinus said:

"Spies of this head!"

The word "head" can mean 1) category, or 2) white-haired.

Sabinus continued:

"So white! So full of years! Well, my most reverend monsters, you may live to see yourselves thus snared."

"Reverend" can mean 1) venerable, or 2) old.

"Away with him!" Opsius said.

"Hale him away," Latiaris said.

"To be a spy for traitors is honorable vigilance," Rufus said.

His words were ambiguous. They could mean that 1) he was spying on behalf of a traitor (Sejanus), or that 2) he was spying out traitors on behalf of a legitimate ruler.

Sabinus said:

"You do well, my most officious instruments of state, men of all uses. Drag me away from here.

"The year is well begun, and I fall fit to be an offering to Sejanus. Go."

Sabinus was referring to himself as a New Year's sacrifice to Sejanus. Normally, no executions were held on the Kalends — the first day — of January.

"Cover him with his garments," Opsius said. "Hide his face."

"There is no need for that," Sabinus said. "Forbear your rude assault. The fault's not shameful that villainy makes a fault."

They exited.

Macro and Caligula talked together.

Macro said:

"Sir, just observe how thick your dangers meet in his — Sejanus' — clear and obvious schemes!

"Your mother and your brothers are now cited to the Senate!

"Their friend Gallus, feasted today by Caesar, has since been committed to prison!

"We met Sabinus here, being hurried to fetters!

"The Senators are all struck with fear and silence, except those whose political hopes depend not on good means but force their private prey from public spoil!

"And you must know that if you stay here, your property and position are sure to be the subject of his hate, as now they are the object."

Now Caligula's property and position are targeted by Sejanus; soon they will belong to Sejanus.

"What would you advise me to do?" Caligula asked.

Macro replied:

"I advise you to go to Capri immediately; and there give up yourself, entirely, to your great-uncle Tiberius.

"Tell Caesar, since your mother is accused, rather than to fly for succors to Augustus' statue, and to the army, with your brethren, you have instead chosen to place your trust in him than to live suspected, or to live in fear each hour that you will be thrust out by bold Sejanus' plots — which you shall confidently state to be most full of peril to the state and Caesar, as the plots are being laid to achieve Sejanus' particular, private ends.

"And you will persuade Tiberius that these plots are not to be allowed to run with common safety."

Emperors were always surrounded by plots as people tried to advance themselves at the expense of others. This plot, however, was different: Sejanus was trying to advance himself at the expense of Tiberius.

Sejanus continued:

"All of this, in support of you, I'll make plain,

"So both shall love and trust with Caesar gain."
Caligula said, "Let's go away, then! Let's prepare ourselves for our journey."
They exited.

Alone, Arruntius, a Senator of good character, prayed:

"Still do thou suffer and tolerate this, heaven? Will no flame, no heat of sin make thy just wrath boil in thy distempered bosom, and overflow the pitchy blazes — smoky fires — of impiety kindled beneath thy throne?

"Can thou still sleep, patient, while vice does make an antic — grotesquely grinning face — at thy dread power, and blow dust and smoke into thy nostrils? Jove, will nothing wake thee?

"Must vile Sejanus pull thee by the beard before thou will open thy black-lidded eye, and kill him with a look?"

Pulling someone's beard was a major insult.

Arruntius continued:

"Well, snore on, dreaming gods, and let this last of that proud giant race heave mountain upon mountain against your state."

Two twin-brother giants — Ephialtes and Otus — attempted to put one mountain on top of another mountain in order to reach the Olympian gods and make war on them. Ephialtes and Otus were Titans: pre-Olympian gods. According to Arruntius, Sejanus is the last of this race of rebelling giants.

Seeing Lepidus, another Senator of integrity, coming toward him, Arruntius said:

"Be good to me, Lady Fortune, and you powers whom I, complaining about you, have profaned.

"I see something that is equal to a prodigy: a great, a noble, and an honest Roman who has lived to be an old man!"

Lepidus walked over to Arruntius.

Arruntius said:

"O Marcus Lepidus, when is our turn to bleed?

"Thyself and I, without our boast — even if we were not the ones to say this — are almost all the few left to be honest in these impious times."

Lepidus replied, "What we are left to be, we will be, Lucius, although tyranny did stare as wide as death to frighten us from it."

"Tyranny has in fact stared as wide as death on Sabinus!" Lucius Arruntius said.

Lepidus was returning from the Gemonian stairs — a staircase — upon the Aventine hill, where the bodies of some executed people were displayed for a few days (and subjected to desecration) before being thrown into the Tiber River or displayed on the bank of the river. The corpse was dragged with a hook and moved from place to place. Lepidus had witnessed the corpse of Sabinus being treated in this way.

Lepidus said about Sabinus, "I saw him now drawn from the Gemonian stairs, and, what increased the direness of the crime, his faithful dog, upbraiding all us Romans, never forsook the corpse, but, seeing it thrown into the stream, leaped in, and drowned with it."

Arruntius said:

"Oh, an act to be envied him by us men!

"We are the next the hook lays hold on, Marcus Lepidus.

"What are thy arts — good patriot, teach them to me — that have preserved thy hairs to this white dye, and kept so reverend and so dear a head safe on its comely shoulders?"

Lepidus replied:

"Arts, Arruntius?

"None but the plain and passive fortitude to suffer and be silent; never stretch these arms against the torrent; live at home, with my own thoughts and innocence about me, not tempting the wolf's jaws: These are my arts."

Lepidus' arts were effective: He lived to be old.

Arruntius said:

"I would begin to study those arts, if I thought they would secure me.

"May I pray to Jove in secret, and be safe? Aye, or aloud? With open wishes? So long as I do not mention Tiberius, or Sejanus?

"Yes, I must mention Tiberius and Sejanus, if I speak out. It is hard, that.

"May I think, and not be tortured by having my limbs pulled out of joint on the rack? What danger is it to dream? Talk in one's sleep? Or cough? Who knows the law?

"May I shake my head, without a comment being made about it?

"May I say that it rains, or that the fair weather continues, and not be thrown upon the Gemonian stairs?

"These now are things on which men's fortune, yea, their fate depends.

"Nothing has privilege against the violent ear that twists the meanings of words. No place, no day, no hour, we see, is free — not even our religious and most sacred times — from one kind of cruelty or another."

New Year's Day was a sacred day, but Sabinus was put to death on that day.

Arruntius continued:

"All matter, nay, any occasion and any pretext will serve to please evil men. Madmen's rage, the idle comments of drunkards, women's meaningless talk, jesters' simplicity — all, all is good that can be seized on.

"Nor is now the end of any person, or for any crime, in doubt; for it is always one and the same: Death, with some little difference of place, or time."

Seeing some people coming toward him, he said, "What's this? Prince Nero? Guarded?"

Laco, the commander of the Night Watch, arrived with Nero, who was guarded by Lictors.

Laco said, "On, Lictors, keep on your way."

He then said to Arruntius and Lepidus:

"My lords, don't speak to him.

"On pain of Caesar's wrath, no man attempt speech with the prisoner."

Nero said to Lepidus and Arruntius:

"Noble friends, be safe. To lose yourselves for words would be as vain hazard to you as it would be small comfort to me.

"Fare you well.

"I wish that all Rome's sufferings in my fate did dwell!"

"Lictors, away!" Laco said.

"Where does Nero go, Laco?" Lepidus asked.

"Sir, he's banished into Pontia, by the Senate," Laco answered.

Arruntius said, "Do I see, and hear, and feel? May I trust my senses? Or does my fantasy — imagination — form it?"

Lepidus asked Laco, "Where's Nero's brother?"

"Drusus Junior is prisoner in the palace," Laco answered.

Nero died in 31 C.E. while in exile on the island of Ponza. Drusus Junior died in prison in 33 C.E. Both Nero and Drusus Junior were starved to death.

Arruntius said:

"Huh. I smell it now; it is rank.

"Where's Agrippina?"

"The princess is confined, at Pandataria, one of the Pontine islands in the Tyrrhenian Sea," Laco said.

Arruntius said:

"Bolts, Vulcan — thunderbolts for Jove! Phoebus, thy bow. Stern Mars, thy sword, and you blue-eyed maiden, thy spear. Thy club, Alcides."

He was swearing.

Vulcan, the blacksmith god, made thunderbolts for Jupiter.

The blue-eyed maiden is Pallas Athena, who is a virgin goddess, and Alcides is another name for Hercules. Alcides means "grandson of Alcaeus." Alcaeus' father was Perseus, so Hercules' great-grandfather is Perseus.

Arruntius continued:

"All the armory of heaven is too little!"

Too little to oppose Sejanus?

Aware that what he said could be used against him, he said:

"To guard the gods, I meant."

He then said:

"Fine, rare dispatch! This same was swiftly borne! Confined? Imprisoned? Banished? Most tripartite!"

In February 1405, Owain Glyndower, Edmund Mortimer, and Henry Percy, 1st Earl of Northumberland signed the Tripartite Indenture, which divided Britain among them if they succeeded in their rebellion against King Henry IV of England.

Arruntius then asked Laco, "What is the reason for Nero's arrest, sir?"

"Treason," Laco answered.

"Oh?" Arrentius said. "The complement of all accusings? That will hit the target, when all else fails."

Lepidus said:

"This turn is strange!

"Just yesterday, the people would not allow even a far less serious crime than treason to be alleged against Nero and Agrippina, but instead they cried out that Caesar's letters accusing Nero and Agrippina were false and forged; that all these plots were malice; and that the ruin of the prince's house — Tiberius' family — was practiced against his knowledge.

"Where are their voices now that they behold his heirs locked up, disgraced, led into exile?"

Arruntius said:

"Their voices are hushed. Drowned in their bellies.

"Wild Sejanus' breath has, like a whirlwind, scattered that poor dust — the people — with this rude blast."

The belly, which feels hunger, is more insistent in its demands than the head is.

Dust is that to which we return after we die.

Arruntius turned to Laco and the others and said:

"We'll talk no treason, sir, if that is what you wait for. Fare you well. We have no need of horse-leeches."

Horse-leeches are literally very large leeches; metaphorically, they are very greedy people.

Arruntius continued:

"Good spy, now that you are spied, begone."

Laco, Nero, and the Lictors exited.

"I fear you wrong him," Lepidus said. "He has the reputation of being an honest Roman."

Arruntius answered:

"And entrusted to this work?

"Lepidus, I'd sooner trust Greek Sinon than a man our state employs."

To end the Trojan War, Ulysses came up with the idea of the Trojan Horse. The Trojan War had been fought for 10 years, and the forces of Agamemnon and the other Greeks had not been able to conquer Troy by might, and so Ulysses had the idea of using trickery to conquer Troy. The Greeks built a huge wooden horse and left it outside Troy, and then they seemed to sail away in their ships and return home. However, the Trojan Horse was hollow and filled with Greek soldiers, including Ulysses and Diomedes, and the ships sailed behind an island so that the Trojans could not see them. A lying Greek named Sinon stayed behind and pretended that he had escaped from Ulysses, who had wanted to kill him. Sinon told the Trojans that if the Trojans were to take the Trojan Horse inside the walls of Troy, then Troy would never fall. Amid great rejoicing, the Trojans took the Trojan Horse inside the walls of Troy. That night, the Greek warriors came out of the Trojan Horse, went to the gates of Troy, killed the Trojan guards, and opened the gates of Troy. Agamemnon and his troops were outside the gates, after returning from hiding behind the island.

The Greeks then conquered Troy, killing many, many Trojans, including Trojan women and children.

Arruntius continued:

"He's gone; and since he is gone, I dare tell you — whom I dare better trust — that our night-eyed Tiberius does not see his minion's drifts; or if he does, he's not as arrant subtle — thoroughly cunning — as we fools take him to be, to breed a mongrel up in his own house with his own blood, and, if the good gods please, encourage him with his own flesh to take a leap at his own throat."

Tiberius had the reputation of being able to see at night immediately after waking up, although his night vision soon faded.

Dogs were encouraged to hunt by being given a piece of the flesh of the animals they hunted. This was called being "fleshed." Sejanus was being "fleshed" with members of Tiberius' own family. Arruntius believed that soon Sejanus could hunt Tiberius.

Arruntius continued:

"I do not beg it, heaven; but if the Fates grant it to these eyes, they must not close."

He would not close his eyes if Sejanus metaphorically tore out Tiberius' throat.

"They must not see it, Lucius Arruntius," Lepidus said.

"Who should prevent them?" Arruntius asked.

"Zeal and duty, with the thought that Tiberius is our prince," Lepidus said.

Arruntius said:

"He is our monster: forfeited to vice so far that no racked — forced out of him — virtue can redeem him.

"His loathed person is fouler than all crimes. He is an emperor only in his lusts; he has retired from all regard of his own reputation, or Rome's, to an obscure island, Capri, where he lives, acting his tragedies while wearing a comic face like a mask appropriate to comedy, amid his rout of Chaldees — that is, astrologers."

Tiberius is thought to have had many sores on his face in his old age.

Arruntius continued:

"Tiberius is spending hours, days, weeks, and months in the unnatural abuse of grave and serious astrology, to the bane — the woe — of men, casting the scope of men's nativities, and, having found anything worthy in their fortune, he kills them, or throws them precipitately in the sea, and boasts that he can mock fate!

"Nay, don't wonder; these are far from the limits of his evil, they are scarcely steps toward the end limit.

"Tiberius has his slaughterhouse at Capri, where he studies murder as an art; and they are dearest in his grace who can devise the deepest tortures.

"Thither, too, he has his boys and beautiful girls taken up out of our noblest houses, the best formed, best nurtured, and most modest. What is good in them serves to provoke his bad. Some are allured, some are threatened; others, detained by their relatives and held back in an attempt to protect them, are kidnapped and taken away by force like captives, and, in sight of their most grieved parents, dealt away to his spintries, sellaries, and slaves, masters of strange and newly invented lusts, for which wise nature has not left a name."

Spintries and sellaries are male prostitutes.

Slaves are servants.

Arruntius continued:

"In addition to this — what most strikes and pierces us and bleeding Rome to the heart — he has, with all his craft, become the ward to his own vassal, a stale catamite, whom he upon our low and suffering necks, has raised from excrement to stand beside the gods, and be sacrificed to in Rome as if he were a god, which Jove beholds, and yet will sooner rive a senseless oak with thunder than his trunk — his body."

According to Arruntius, Tiberius had metaphorically become the ward of Sejanus, who had been a catamite: a boy used for homosexual sex. Arruntius may also be saying that Tiberius is now Sejanus' catamite.

One can wonder whether Trump is Putin's catamite.

Although Jupiter has witnessed this and has witnessed Sejanus' rise to power and misuse of that power, Jupiter still refrains from striking Sejanus with a lightning bolt.

Laco, Pomponius, and Minutius entered the scene.

Pomponius and Minutius were followers of Sejanus.

Laco, Pomponius, and Minutius talked among themselves, while Arruntius and Lepidus observed them from some distance away and commented privately on them.

"These letters make men doubtful what to expect, whether Tiberius' coming back to Rome, or his death," Laco said.

Tiberius' letters sometimes said that he was well and would soon return to Rome, and they sometimes said that he was deathly ill and unable to return to Rome.

Pomponius said, "True, both — and whichever comes soonest, thank the gods for it."

Arruntius said quietly to Lepidus, "Listen, their talk is about Caesar. I would hear all voices."

Minutius said, "One day, he's well, and will return to Rome. The next day, he is sick, and does not know when to hope for his return."

Laco said, "True, and today, one of Sejanus' friends was honored by special writ; and on the next morning another of Sejanus' friends was punished —"

"— by more special writ," Pomponius said.

Minutius said:

"One man receives Tiberius' praises of Sejanus. A second man receives a letter with only slight mention of Sejanus. A third man receives a letter with no mention of Sejanus. A fourth man receives a letter with rebukes of Sejanus.

"And thus Tiberius leaves the Senate divided and suspended, all uncertain."

Laco said:

"These forked — saying one thing and then saying the opposite thing — tricks, I don't understand them.

"I wish that he would tell us whom he loves or hates, so that we might follow, without fear or doubt!"

Arruntius said quietly to Lepidus, "Good heliotrope! Is this your honest man? Let him be yours so still. To me, he is a knave and a scoundrel."

Literally, a heliotrope is a plant that turns its flowers to face the sun. Figuratively, a heliotrope is a person who serves people who are waxing and deserts people who are waning.

Pomponius said:

"I cannot tell whom to follow.

"Sejanus still goes on, and mounts higher, we see. New statues of Sejanus are proposed, fresh pages of titles, large inscriptions read, his fortune is sworn by, he himself newly gone out as Caesar's colleague in the fifth Consulship. More altars smoke to him than all the gods.

"What more would he wish for?"

Arruntius said to himself, "That the dear smoke of the altars would choke him. That is what I would wish more for Sejanus."

"Peace, good Arruntius," Lepidus said quietly.

"But there are letters come, they say, even now, which do forbid that last," Laco said. "The letters forbid sacrifices to any human being."

"Do you hear so?" Minutius asked.

"Yes," Laco said.

"By Pollux, that's the worst," Pomponius said.

"By Hercules, that's the best!" Arruntius said to himself.

"I did not like the sign, when Regulus, whom we all know is no friend to Sejanus, did, by Tiberius' so precise command, succeed a fellow in the Consulship. It boded somewhat," Minutius said.

Pomponius said, "Not a mote. Regulus' partner, Fulcinius Trio, is Sejanus' own follower, and loyal to him."

Tiberius and Sejanus were *Consules ordinarii* who were appointed at the beginning of the year.

Regulus and Fulcinius Trio were *Consules suffecti* who held office during the second part of 31 C.E. They took office when, as became the custom during the reign of Caesar Augustus, the *Consules ordinarii* resigned their office partway during their Consulships so that others could share the honor of being Consul.

Regulus, who was not friendly to Sejanus, was appointed to office at the command of Tiberius.

Fulcinius Trio was a follower of Sejanus.

Seeing Terentius coming toward them, Pomponius said, "Here comes Terentius. He can give us more information."

Terentius walked over to them.

Pomponius, Minutius, and Laco talked quietly with Terentius.

Lepidus and Arruntius, still standing apart, conversed together.

Lepidus said:

"I'll never believe anything except that Caesar has some scent of bold Sejanus' footing [dancing, established place]. These cross-points [crossing the feet in dancing, devious plots] of varying letters and opposing Consuls, mingling his honors and his punishments, feigning now ill, now well, raising

Sejanus and then depressing him, as now of late in all reports we have it, cannot be empty of scheming.

"It is Tiberius' art.

"Tiberius has found his favorite grown too great, and, with his greatness, strong, so that all the soldiers of the Praetorian Guard have been, with their leaders, made devoted and loyal to him, so that almost all the Senate are his creatures or are mainly dependent on him, either by reason of benefit, or hope, or fear.

"Tiberius has lost much of his own patronage by sharing his power with Sejanus.

"Tiberius, by the increase of his rank lusts and rages has quite disarmed himself of love or other public means to dare an open contestation.

"Therefore, Tiberius' subtlety has chosen this doubling line — manipulating Sejanus this way and then that — to hold Sejanus always in check: not so much to frighten Sejanus as to wholly put him out and make him uncertain, and yet check his farther boldness.

"In the meantime, by his employments of Sejanus, Tiberius makes him odious to the staggering, fickle crowd, whose aid in the end Tiberius hopes to use, as dependable, who, when they hold sway, bear down, and overturn all objects in their way."

Tiberius was able to withdraw support from Sejanus by being fickle in his praise and dispraise of him. Since the Romans did not know whether Sejanus was in or out of favor with Tiberius, many Romans did not openly support or not support him but waited until they could find out whether or not Tiberius supported him. Tiberius also gave Sejanus tasks to perform that made him unpopular.

Arruntius said, "You may be a Lynceus, Lepidus, yet I can see no reason why a politic tyrant, who can so well disguise it, should not have taken a nearer way: pretended to be honest and loyal to Sejanus, and come home to cut Sejanus' throat, by law."

Lynceus was a sharp-sighted Argonaut of Jason and the Argonauts fame. He was reputed to be able to see objects that were underground.

Lepidus said, "Aye, but Tiberius' fear would never be masked, although his vices were."

The clients of Sejanus had been whispering among themselves. Now their voices became louder.

Lepidus and Arruntius listened to them.

"His Lordship then is still in grace?" Pomponius said.

"I assure you, he had never been in more, either of grace or of power," Terentius said.

"The gods are wise and just," Pomponius said.

Arruntius said to himself, "The fiends they are, to suffer thee to belie them!"

Arruntius was cynical, and he wondered why the gods had not punished such an evil person as Pomponius for saying that they were wise and just.

If the gods were wise and just, would Sejanus have so much power?

Terentius showed Pomponius, Minutius, and Laco some letters and said, "I have here his last and present letters, where Tiberius writes and calls him the 'partner of his cares' and 'his Sejanus' —"

Laco asked, "But is it true that it is prohibited to sacrifice to Sejanus?"

Terentius answered, "Some such thing Caesar makes scruple of, but he does not forbid it, no more than to himself; he says that he could wish that making sacrifices to human beings were desisted from by all."

"Is it no other?" Laco said. "Is that how it is?"

"No other, on my trust," Terentius said. "For your better assurance, here is that letter, too."

He showed them that letter from Tiberius.

Arruntius said quietly:

"How easily do wretched men believe what they would have! When men really want to believe something, they will believe it on little evidence."

He then asked Lepidus, "Does this look like a plot by Tiberius?"

Lepidus said quietly, "Noble Arruntius, wait."

Laco looked at the letter and said, "Tiberius names Sejanus here without adding Sejanus' titles."

As a mark of respect, people would mention other people's titles.

Lepidus said quietly to Arruntius, "Note that."

Arruntius replied quietly, "Yes, and if I take note of what Laco says, I will come off — turn out to be — a notable fool. I will, indeed."

"Tiberius addresses him as no other than Sejanus," Laco said. "No titles are mentioned at all."

"That's but haste in him who writes," Pomponius said. "Here Tiberius gives large amends."

He showed the others another letter from Tiberius.

"And with his own handwriting?" Minutius asked.

"Yes," Pomponius said.

"Indeed?" Laco said.

Terentius replied, "Believe it, gentlemen, Sejanus' breast has never received more full contentments than in this letter at this present time."

Pomponius asked, "Does Sejanus take well the escape of young Caligula with Macro?"

Caligula was on the island of Capri with Tiberius.

Terentius replied, "Indeed, at the first airing of that escape — when the escape first became known — it somewhat troubled him."

Lepidus said quietly to Arruntius, "Do you see this?"

Arruntius replied quietly, "This is nothing. Riddles. Until I *see* Sejanus struck down, no rumor about his downfall strikes — affects — me."

Some of us have said the same thing about Trump and Putin.

Arruntius and Lepidus exited.

"I don't like it," Pomponius said. "I wonder why Sejanus would not attempt something — a rebellion — against Tiberius during Sejanus' Consulship, seeing the people begin to favor Caligula."

Terentius said, "He now repents not rebelling then, but he's employed Pagonianus to follow Caligula; and he holds that correspondence — that communication — there with all who are near and close around Caesar, in such a way that no thought — no scheme — can pass without his knowledge from there to become an act to confront and threaten him."

"I welcome the news," Pomponius said.

"But how did Macro come to be so trusted by and in favor with Caligula?" Laco asked.

Pomponius answered, "Oh, sir, Macro has a wife, and the young prince Caligula has an appetite. Macro can look up and spy flies in the roof when there are fleas in bed, and he has a learned nose to assure his sleeps."

Macro can ignore things near him and keep an eye on things that are away from him. He can sleep soundly because he has a nose that scents what he needs to know to sleep soundly. Such skills ensure that he will ignore the affair of his wife with Caligula.

Pomponius continued, "Who, to be favored of the rising sun, would not lend a little of the waning moon? It is the safest ambition."

The rising sun is Caligula, and Macro's wife is the waning moon.

Pomponius then said, "Noble Terentius!"

Terentius said, "The night grows fast upon us. At your service."

All present exited.

At this point in Ben Jonson's play, a Chorus of Musicians performed.

CHAPTER 5

— 5.1 —

Alone, Sejanus said to himself:

"Swell, swell, my joys, and don't be afraid to declare yourselves as ample as your causes are.

"I did not live until now, this my first hour, wherein I see my power reach my thoughts. Just this one final thing, and I will seize my wishes.

"Great, and high, the world knows only two. That's Rome, and I. My roof does not receive me — I have risen above it; it is air I tread — and, at each step, I feel my advanced — raised high — head knock out a star in heaven!"

Sejanus had risen above his house: his family. He was not a member of the highest social class, but he had grown to be the second most important person in the Roman world, and he believed that he soon would be the first most important person in that world.

Sejanus continued:

"Reared to this height, all my desires now seem modest, poor, and slight, which previously sounded impudent. It is place, not blood, that discerns and distinguishes the noble and the base.

"Isn't there something more than to be Caesar?"

Using the royal plural, Sejanus continued:

"Must we rest there? It irks to have come so far, to be so near a standstill.

"Caligula, we wish that thou would stand steadfast and resolute, and many of you, in our way!

"Winds lose their strength when they fly empty, unmet by woods or buildings; great fires die when they lack matter to withstand them.

"So it is our grief, and it will be our loss, to know our power shall lack opponents, unless the gods, by mixing in the cause, would bless our fortune with our conquest of them.

"That would be worth Sejanus' strife, if the Fates dared but bring it forth."

Sejanus wanted the gods to oppose him because he would gain great glory by defeating them.

Terentius and a servant entered the scene.

"May great Sejanus be safe!" Terentius said.

"What is it now, Terentius?" Sejanus asked.

"Hasn't my lord heard the wonder?" Terentius asked.

"No," Sejanus said. "Tell me what it is."

"The news is violent in the mouths of people I meet who run, in mobs, to Pompey's Theater to view your statue, which, they say, sends forth a smoke as from a furnace, black and dreadful," Terentius said.

"Some traitor has put fire in the statue," Sejanus replied.

He then said to a servant, "You, go and see. And let the head of the statue be taken off, to see what is inside."

The servant exited.

Sejanus said, "Some slave has practiced an imposture and deception to stir up and excite the people."

Satrius, Natta, and the servant entered the scene. Satrius and Natta were clients of Sejanus.

"What is it now?" Sejanus asked.

He asked the servant, "Why do you return?"

Satrius said, "The head, my lord, already has been taken off. I saw it; and, at the opening, there leapt out a great and monstrous serpent!"

"Monstrous!" Sejanus said. "Why? Did it have a beard? And horns? No heart? A tongue as forked as flattery? Did it have the hue of such men as live in great men's bosoms — who live under the protection of great men? Was the spirit of it Macro's?"

Natta answered, "May it please the most divine Sejanus, in my days — and by his sacred Fortune I affirm it — I have not seen a more extended and reached-out, grown, foul, spotted, venomous, ugly —"

"Oh, the Fates!" Sejanus said. "What a wild muster's here of attributes, to describe a worm, a snake!"

"But how should that come there, my lord!" Terentius said.

"What!" Sejanus said. "And you, too, Terentius? I think you mean to make it a prodigy — an ill omen — in your reporting."

"Can the wise Sejanus think that heaven has meant it to mean less?" Terentius replied.

"Oh, superstition!" Sejanus said. "Why, then the falling of our couch, which broke this morning because it was burdened with the populous weight of our clients waiting to salute and greet us, or the running of the cat between our legs, as we set forth to go to the Capitol, were also prodigies."

Terentius said:

"I think that they are ominous, and I wish that they had not happened!

"As, today, the fate of some of your servants, who, diverting from their way, not able to follow you because of the throng of people, slipped down the Gemonian stairs and broke their necks.

"Besides, in taking your last augury, no prosperous, auspicious bird appeared, but croaking ravens — birds of ill omen — flew unsteadily, and from the sacrifice flew to the prison, where they sat, all night, beating the air with sounds from their obstreperous and noisy beaks.

"I dare not counsel, but I could entreat great Sejanus to try to move the gods, once more, with sacrifice."

Sejanus said:

"What excellent fools religion makes of men!

"Does Terentius believe that if these were dangers, as I shame to think them to be, that the gods could change the certain course of fate?

"Or, if they could, that they would — now, in a moment — for the sacrificial fat from an ox, or less, be bribed to invert those old decrees?

"If so, then think that the gods, like flies, are to be captivated with the steam of flesh or blood diffused about their altars; think that their power is as cheap as I esteem it small.

"Of all the throng of gods who fill the hall of Mount Olympus, and, without pity, lade the back of poor Atlas, who holds up the sky, I don't know even one deity other than Fortune to whom I would throw up, in begging smoke, even one grain of incense, or whose ear I'd buy with thus much oil.

"Lady Fortune I indeed adore, and I keep her pleasing image in my house, an image previously belonging to a Roman King, but now called mine, as by the better style."

Sejanus believed that he had a better style — title — than the old Roman Kings, and so he was a better owner of the statue of Lady Fortune.

Sejanus continued:

"I don't care if, just for satisfying your scrupulous — distrustful and anxious — fantasies, I offer a sacrifice to Lady Fortune.

"Tell our priest to prepare for us honey, milk, and poppy, his masculine —
strong — incense on the altar, and his night vestments. Say that our rites are
pressing and are to be performed immediately.

"Once these rites are performed, you'll see how vain, and how worthy of
laughter, your fears are."

They exited.

— 5.2 —

Cotta and Pomponius met each other and talked together.

Pomponius was a follower of Sejanus, and Cotta was a man without scruples.

"Pomponius! Where are you going so speedily?" Cotta asked.

Pomponius replied, "I go to give my lord Sejanus notice —"

"Notice of what?" Cotta asked.

"Of Macro," Pomponius answered.

"Has he come back to Rome?" Cotta asked.

"He entered just now the house of Regulus," Pomponius answered.

"The Consul opposing Sejanus?" Cotta asked.

"Some half-hour ago," Pomponius said.

"And by night, too!" Cotta said. "Wait, sir. I'll bear you company."

"Come along, then," Pomponius said.

They exited.

Macro and Regulus talked together. A servant was present.

Macro said to Regulus, "It is Caesar's will to have a fully attended Senate, and therefore your edict must lay a deep mulct — a heavy fine — on such as shall be absent."

"So my edict does," Regulus said.

He told the servant, "Bear it to my fellow Consul to subscribe and add his name to it."

Macro said to the servant, "And tell him it must be proclaimed early; the place is Apollo's temple."

The servant exited.

"That's remembered," Regulus said.

"And the edict must say at what hour," Macro said.

"Yes," Regulus said.

Macro asked, "Did you forget to send someone for the Provost of the Watch — for Laco?"

"I have not," Regulus said. "Here he comes."

Laco entered the scene.

Macro said, "Gracinus Laco, you are a friend most welcome. By and by I'll speak with you."

He then said to Regulus, "You must procure for me this list of the Praetorian cohorts, with the names of the Centurions, and their Tribunes."

Tiberius had secretly placed these soldiers under the command of Macro.

"Aye," Regulus replied.

Macro said to Laco, "I bring you letters and a wish for your good prosperity from Caesar. "

"Sir, both are welcome," Laco said.

Macro said to Regulus, "And listen, with your note, find for me those men who are the eminent men, and the men most of action."

"That shall be done for you, too," Regulus said.

Macro turned to Laco and said, "Most worthy Laco, Caesar salutes you."

Regulus, the Consul, exited.

Turning back to where Regulus had been, Macro said, "Consul! Death and Furies! Gone now?"

He said to Laco, "The theme of my conversation will please you, sir."

He called, "Ho! Regulus?"

He then said, "May the anger of the gods follow his diligent legs and overtake them in the likeness of the gout!"

Gout is a disease that causes acute pain, especially in the feet.

Regulus returned.

Macro said to him, "Oh, my good lord, we lacked your presence. I want you to send another man to Fulcinius Trio, who supports Sejanus, straightaway, to tell him you will come and speak with him — the content of what you will speak to him about we'll devise — to keep him there and out of the way, while I, with Laco, survey the soldiers of the Watch."

While Macro turned to Laco, Regulus exited again.

Macro asked Laco, "What are your strengths in soldiers, Gracinus?"

Gracinus Laco answered, "Seven cohorts."

Cohorts are military units of a Roman legion. Cohorts today would be called battalions.

Turning back to where Regulus had been, Macro said:

"You see what Caesar writes, and — gone again?

"Regulus surely has a vein of swift-winged Mercury in his feet."

He asked Laco, "Do you know what store of the Praetorian soldiers Sejanus holds about him for his bodyguard?"

Laco answered, "I don't know the exact number — but I think three centuries."

A century is a unit originally of 100 soldiers, but at this time the usual number was 80 soldiers.

"Three?" Macro said. "Good."

"Three at most, not four," Laco said.

"And who are those Centurions?" Macro asked.

"That the Consul Regulus can best inform you," Laco said.

"When he's away?" Macro said sarcastically. "A spite on his nimble industry!"

He then asked, "Gracinus, do you find in these letters what place you hold in the trust of royal Caesar?"

Gracinus Laco answered, "Aye, and I am —"

Macro interrupted, "Sir, the honors there proposed are but beginnings of his great favors."

Laco began, "They are more —"

Macro interrupted, "I heard him when he did study what to add."

Laco said, "— my life, and all I hold —"

Macro interrupted, "You were his own first choice, which does confirm as much as you can speak; and this plan of action will, if we succeed, make more."

He then asked, "Your guards are seven cohorts, you say?"

"Yes," Laco answered.

"Those we must hold still in readiness, and undischarged," Macro said.

"I understand so much," Laco said. "But how can it —"

Macro interrupted, "— be done without suspicion, you'll object?"

Regulus returned and asked, "What's that?"

Laco answered, "The keeping of the Night Watch in arms when morning comes."

Macro said, "The Senate shall be met, and shall be set so early in the temple, that all notice of the Night Watch in arms will be avoided."

Regulus said, "If we need to, we have the commission to possess the palace, free Prince Drusus, and make him our chief."

Drusus Junior was imprisoned in the palace. If Sejanus were to summon armed men, then Drusus Junior would be freed and placed at the head of Tiberius' armed men.

Macro said to himself, "That secret would have burnt his reverend mouth, had he not spit it out now."

Regulus had said something that Macro wished he had not said.

Macro said to Regulus:

"By the gods, you carry things, too. You have responsibilities.

"Let me borrow a man or two, to bear these —"

Regulus exited.

Macro said to Laco, "That idea of freeing Drusus Caesar is projected as the last, and utmost — the last resort; it is not otherwise to be remembered."

Regulus returned with some servants.

"Here are servants," he said.

Giving letters to the servants, Macro said:

"Carry these to Arruntius, these to Lepidus, this letter bear to Cotta, this one to Latiaris.

"If they ask you about me, say that I have taken a fresh horse and departed."

The servants exited.

Macro said to Regulus:

"You, my lord, go to your colleague the Consul Fulcinius Trio, and be sure to hold him there with a long narration of the new fresh favors meant to be given Sejanus, his great patron.

"I, with trusted Laco here, will go to the guards.

"So then, let us separate from each other.

"For night has many eyes,

"Whereof, although most do sleep, yet some are spies."

Trumpeters, flautists, Heralds, a Priest, Attendants, Sejanus, Terentius, Satrius, Natta, etc., met together in Sejanus' house.

The First Herald said loudly, "Everything profane be far from here! Fly, fly far off. Be absent a far distance. Far from here be all profane."

Heralds preceded the Priest to keep away all profane things from him and the sacrifice. Participants in the ritual were also supposed to keep away all profane thoughts.

The trumpeters and flautists sounded while the Priest washed as part of the ritual.

The Priest said, "We have been faulty, but we repent us now, and we bring pure hands, pure vestments, and pure minds."

As part of the ritual, the Priest repented his sins.

"Pure vessels," the First Minister said.

"And pure offerings," the Second Minister said.

"Pure garlands," the Third Minister said.

The Priest said, "Bestow your garlands, and, with reverence, place the vervin on the altar."

Vervin are branches of such trees as laurel, myrtle, olive, and cypress.

"Favor your tongues!" the First Herald said loudly. "Be silent!"

One reason for silence was to avoid saying any words of ill omen.

The Priest prayed to Lady Fortune: "Great mother Fortune, Queen of human state, rectress — female ruler — of action, arbitress of fate, to whom all sway, all power, all empire bows, be present, and be propitious to our vows!"

"Favor it with your tongues!" the First Herald said loudly. "Be silent!"

"Be present, and be propitious to our vows!" the First Minister said.

The trumpeters and the flautists sounded again.

The Priest took up some of the honey with his finger and tasted it, and then he ministered to all the rest. He did the same with the milk; in an earthen vessel, he dealt the milk around him.

This done, he sprinkled milk upon the altar, then imposed the honey, and kindled and inflamed his aromatic gums, and after swinging his censer about the altar to perfume it, he placed his censer thereon, into which they put several branches of poppy.

"Gums" are aromatic substances — incense — that are burned in the censer.

The music ceased, and the Priest said, "Accept our offering, and be pleased, great goddess."

"See, see, the image stirs!" Terentius said.

"And it turns away!" Satrius said.

"Lady Fortune averts her face!" Natta said.

The statue of Lady Fortune had turned her face away from the sacrifice.

The Priest said:

"Avert, you gods, the bad omen."

Lady Fortune continued to look away from the sacrifice.

The Priest continued:

"Still! Still! We have neglected some pious rite."

Lady Fortune continued to look away from the sacrifice.

The Priest continued:

"Yet!

"Heaven, be appeased, and let all the tokens — the divine signs — be false, or void, that speak thy present wrath!"

Sejanus said:

"Be thou dumb, fearful Priest. Be silent, and gather up thyself, with these thy wares, which I, in spite of thy blind mistress, or thy juggling mystery and cheating, deceiving trade, religion, throw thus, scorned, on the earth."

Sejanus swept the altar clean.

He addressed the statue:

"Nay, hold thy look averted, until I woo thee to turn again; and thou shall stand to all posterity the eternal object of mockery and laughter, with thy neck writhed to thy tail and turned backwards like a ridiculous cat.

He ordered:

"Clear away these fumes, these superstitious lights, and all these cozening, duping ceremonies — you, your pure and spiced — over-scrupulous and over-delicate — conscience!"

The Priest, trumpeters, flautists, Heralds, attendants, etc. picked up the sacrificial items and exited.

Sejanus, Terentius, Satrius, and Natta remained.

Sejanus said:

"I — the slave and mock of fools who scorn my worthy head — I have been titled and adored as a god, yea, and been sacrificed unto, myself, in Rome, no less than Jove — and I am brought to do rites to a peevish giglot — a peevish wanton woman?

"Perhaps the thought and shame of that made Fortune turn her face, knowing herself the lesser deity, and only my servant.

"Bashful Queen, if that is so, Sejanus thanks thy modesty."

Seeing some men coming he asked, "Who's that?"

Pomponius and Minutius entered the scene.

Pomponius said to Minutius, "His fortune suffers until he hears my news. I've waited here too long."

He then said to Sejanus, "Macro, my lord —"

Sejanus said, "Speak lower, and withdraw with me."

Sejanus took Pomponius aside. The others conversed while Sejanus and Pomponius conferred privately.

"Are these things true?" Terentius asked.

"Thousands are gazing at it, in the streets," Minutius answered.

Returning from his conference with Pomponius, Sejanus asked, "What's that?"

Terentius said, "Minutius tells us here, my lord, that, a new head being set upon your statue, a rope has since been found wreathed about it; and, just now, a fiery meteor, in the form of a great ball, was seen to roll along the troubled air, where yet it hangs, its flight unfinished, the amazing wonder of the multitude!"

"No more," Sejanus said. "That Macro's come is more ominous than all these other things!"

"Has Macro come?" Terentius asked.

"I saw him," Pomponius said.

"Where?" Terentius asked. "With whom?"

"With Regulus," Pomponius said.

Sejanus said, "Terentius —"

"My lord?" Terentius said.

Sejanus ordered, "Send for the military Tribunes. We will immediately have more of the soldiers sent up for our bodyguard."

Terentius exited.

Sejanus said, "Minutius, we want you to go for Cotta, Latiaris, Trio the Consul, and whatever other Senators you know are sure and are on our side."

Minutius exited.

Sejanus ordered, "You, my good Natta, go for Laco, Provost of the Watch."

Natta exited.

Sejanus said, "Now, Satrius, the time of proof comes on. Arm all our servants, and do it without tumult."

Satrius exited.

Sejanus ordered, "You, Pomponius, hold some good conversation with the Consul Regulus. Attempt to influence him to be on our side, noble friend."

Pomponius exited.

Alone, Sejanus said to himself:

"These things begin to look like dangers, now, that are worthy of my fates.

"Lady Fortune, I see thy worst. Let doubtful states of affairs and uncertain things hang upon thy will. Surest death shall render me a certain accounting still.

"Yet why is now my thought turned toward death, when I am a man whom the Fates have let go on so far in breath, unchecked and unreproved?

"I am the man who helped to fell the lofty cedar of the world: Germanicus.

"I am the man who, at one stroke, cut down Drusus Senior, that upright elm; withered his vine — his wife, Livia; laid Silius and Sabinus, two strong oaks, flat on the earth; besides those other shrubs — insignificant people — Cordus and Sosia, Claudia Pulchra, Furnius and Gallus, which I have grubbed up and uprooted; and since have set my axe so strong and deep into the root of spreading Agrippina; lopped off and scattered her proud branches, Nero, Drusus Junior, and Caius Caligula, too, although replanted —"

Caligula was replanted on the island of Capri, where was the Emperor Tiberius.

Sejanus continued:

"If it is your will, Destinies — the three Fates — that, after all this, I faint now, before I touch my goal, you are just cruel; and I already have done things great enough."

The three Fates determined the length of mortal lives.

Sejanus continued:

"All Rome has been my slave. The Senate sat and was an idle onlooker and witness of my power, when I have blushed and was ashamed more to command it than to suffer it."

The Senate had approved whatever Sejanus wanted. Sejanus could have asked for more things for the Senate to approve, but he was ashamed to ask for more, having gotten so much already.

Sejanus continued:

"All the Senate fathers have sat ready and prepared to give me empire, temples, or their throats, when I would ask for them. And, what crowns the top, Rome, Senate, people, all the world have seen Jove as just my equal, Caesar as just my second.

"It is then your malice, Fates, who, except your own,

"Envy and fear to have any power long known."

Terentius and some Tribunes stood together.

Terentius said to the Tribunes, "Stay here. I'll tell His Lordship that you have come."

"His Lordship" was Sejanus.

Minutius, Cotta, and Latiaris, all of whom were carrying letters from Tiberius, entered the scene.

Latiaris supported Sejanus. Cotta was a Senator without scruples.

Minutius said, "Marcus Terentius, please tell my lord that here are Cotta and Latiaris."

"Sir, I shall," Terentius said.

He exited.

Cotta and Latiaris conferred over and compared their letters.

Cotta said, "My letter is the very same as yours; it only requires me to be present there, and to give my voice — my vote — to strengthen Tiberius' design."

"Doesn't he name what it is?" Latiaris asked.

"No, nor does he name it to you," Cotta said.

"It is strange, and singularly ambiguous!" Latiaris said.

"So it is!" Cotta said. "It may be the case that all has been left to Lord Sejanus."

Natta and Laco entered the scene.

"Gentlemen, where's my lord?" Natta asked.

"We await him here," a Tribune said.

"The Provost Laco?" Cotta said. "What's the news?"

Latiaris began, "My lord —"

He was interrupted by the arrival of Sejanus and Terentius.

Sejanus said:

"Now, my right dear, noble, and trusted friends. How much I am a captive to your kindness!

"Most worthy Cotta, Latiaris; Laco, give me your valiant hand; and gentlemen, give me your loves.

"I wish I could divide myself unto you; or I could wish that it lay within our" — he was using the majestic plural — "narrow powers to give satisfaction to you for your so enlarged bounty to me.

"Gracinus Laco, we much ask you, hold your guards undischarged when morning comes."

He then asked Minutius:

"Did you see the Consul?"

"Trio will very quickly be here, my lord," Minutius answered.

"They are just giving orders for the edict to officially summon the Senate," Cotta said.

The two Consuls were telling the Senators to assemble.

"What! The Senate?" Sejanus said.

Normally, he would know all the doings of the Senate.

"Yes," Latiaris said. "This morning, in Apollo's temple."

"We are ordered by letter to be there, my lord," Cotta said.

"By letter?" Sejanus said. "Please let me see the letter."

Latiaris whispered to Cotta, "Doesn't His Lordship know about this?"

"His Lordship" was Sejanus.

Cotta whispered back, "It seems that he doesn't!"

"A Senate ordered to assemble?" Sejanus said. "Without my knowledge? And this suddenly? Senators by letters required to be there! Who brought these?"

"Macro," Cotta answered.

"My enemy!" Sejanus said. "And when?"

"This midnight," Cotta said.

Sejanus said, "Time, along with every other circumstance, shows that it has some strain of plot in it!"

Seeing Satrius coming, he said, "What is the news now?"

Satrius entered the scene, and Sejanus and he talked together privately.

Satrius said to Sejanus, "My lord, Sertorius Macro is outside, alone, and he requests to have a private conference about business of high nature with Your Lordship, he says to me. This business much regards and affects you."

"Let him come here," Sejanus said.

"It is better, my lord, to withdraw," Satrius advised. "You will betray what number and strength of friends are now about you, which information he comes here to spy and learn."

"Isn't he armed?" Sejanus asked.

"We'll search him," Satrius said.

Sejanus ordered, "No, but take and lead him to some room where you, concealed, may keep a guard upon us."

Satrius exited.

Sejanus then said, "Noble Laco, you are our trust, and until our own cohorts can be brought up, your strengths must be our guard."

He then spoke humbly to his supporters: "Now, good Minutius, honored Latiaris, most worthy, and my most unwearied friends, I will return very quickly."

He exited.

"Most worthy lord!" Latiaris said.

"His Lordship has suddenly turned kind, I think," Cotta said. "I have not observed it in him heretofore."

"It is true, and it becomes him nobly," the First Tribune said.

"I am enraptured with it," Minutius said.

"By Mars, he has my lives, even if they were a million, for this single grace," the Second Tribune said.

"Aye, and to call a man by some title!" Laco said.

Sejanus had called them "good Minutius, honored Latiaris, most worthy, and my most unwearied friends."

"As he did me!" Latiaris said.

"And me!" Minutius said.

"Who would not spend his life and fortunes to purchase but the look of such a lord?" Latiaris said.

Laco said to himself, "He who would be neither a lord's fool nor the world's."

Sejanus, Macro, and Satrius were in a room together.

Sejanus said, "Macro! Most welcome, as my most desired and wished-for friend! Let me enjoy my longings. When did you arrive?"

"About the noon of night," Macro said.

Sejanus said, "Satrius, allow us to speak alone."

Satrius exited and then concealed himself in a place where he could watch and guard Sejanus.

Macro said, "I have been, since I came, with both the Consuls, Regulus and Trio, on a private mission from Caesar."

"How fares it with our great and royal master?" Sejanus asked.

Macro answered:

"Right plentifully well, as with a prince who still extends the great proportion of his large favors to the man whom his judgment has already made once divine choice — like the god who does not fail nor is wearied to bestow his bounty on the man whose merit deserves it, as merit does in you, already the most happy, and, before the sun shall climb the south, the most high Sejanus.

"Let not my lord be amazed. For to this end was I by Caesar sent for, to come to the isle of Capri, where he is, with special caution to conceal my journey; and from there I had my dispatch as privately again to Rome. I was ordered to come here by night, and only to the Consuls make narration of his great purpose, so that the benefit might come fuller and more striking by how much it was less looked for or aspired by you, or least given form in the common thought."

"What may this be?" Sejanus asked. "You are part of myself, my soulmate, dear Macro! If it is good, speak out and share it with your Sejanus."

Macro said:

"If it were bad, I should forever loathe myself to be the messenger to so good a lord.

"I exceed my instructions by acquainting your Lordship with thus much; but I am willing to rely on your wise secrecy and prudent silence, and I do this because I would have no apprehensive fear molest or rack your peace of thought.

"For I assure you, my noble lord, that no Senator yet knows the business meant, though all, by separate letters, are told to be there and give their votes, only to add to the state and grace — dignity and favor — of what is purposed."

"You take pleasure, Macro, like a coy wench, in torturing your devoted friend," Sejanus said. "What can be worth this suffering?"

Macro said, "That which follows, the tribunicial power that you, Sejanus, are to have this day conferred upon you, and by public Senate."

Macro was saying that Sejanus would get the *tribunicia potestas*, which would mark him as the heir to Tiberius. A person with the tribunicial power could veto Senatorial decrees and could propose laws, and his person was inviolable.

"Lady Fortune, be mine again!" Sejanus said. "Thou have answered sufficiently and given satisfaction for thy imagined disloyalty."

"My lord, I have no longer time," Macro said. "The day approaches, and I must go back to Caesar."

"Where's Caligula?" Sejanus asked.

Most people would have assumed that Caligula would be the successor to Tiberius.

Macro said:

"That I forgot to tell Your Lordship.

"Why, he lingers yonder, about Capri, disgraced. Tiberius has not seen him yet.

"Caligula would have insisted on thrusting himself to go with me, against my wish and will, but I have repaid his presumptuous trouble with as reluctant a response as my neglect or silence could afford him.

"Your Lordship cannot now command me anything because I take no knowledge that I saw you, but I shall boast to live to serve Your Lordship, and so I take my leave."

"Honest and worthy Macro, your love and friendship," Sejanus said.

He called, "Who's there?"

Satrius showed himself.

Sejanus said, "Satrius, attend my honorable friend as he goes forth."

Macro and Satrius exited, leaving Sejanus alone.

Sejanus said to himself:

"Oh, how vain and vile a passion is this fear! What base, uncomely things it makes men do!

"Suspect their noblest friends, as I did this man, Macro, flatter poor enemies, entreat their servants, stoop, court, and catch at the benevolence of creatures to whom, within this hour, I would not have vouchsafed a quarter-look — a contemptuous sidelong glance — or the sight of a piece of my face!

"You, whom fools call gods, hang all the sky with your prodigious signs, fill earth with monsters, drop the Scorpion down out of the zodiac, or the fiercer Lion — Leo — shake off the loosened globe from her long hinge — the long axle of the earth — roll all the world in darkness, and let loose the enraged winds to turn up groves and towns!

"When I fear again, let me be struck with forked fire — lightning — and unpitied die.

"He who fears, is worthy of calamity."

Terentius, Minutius, Laco, Cotta, Latiaris, some Tribunes, and others met Pomponius and the two Consuls: Regulus and Trio.

"Isn't my lord here?" Pomponius asked about Sejanus.

"Sir, he will be here very soon," Terentius answered.

Cotta asked Trio the Consul quietly, "What is the news, Fulcinius Trio?"

They held a hushed conversation.

Trio answered:

"Good, good tidings, but keep it to yourself.

"My lord Sejanus is to receive this day, in open Senate, the tribunicial power."

"Is it true?" Cotta asked.

"No words — do not give voice to your thought — but sir, believe it," Trio answered.

Latiaris joined in this hushed conversation.

"What does the Consul say?" Latiaris asked.

"Don't tell anyone," Cotta said. "He tells me that today my lord Sejanus —"

Trio interrupted, "— I must entreat you, Cotta, on your honor not to reveal it."

"On my life, sir," Cotta said.

"Say it," Latiaris said.

Cotta did:

"— is to receive the tribunicial power.

"But as you are an honorable man, let me conjure you not to utter it, for that information was entrusted to me with that condition."

"I am Harpocrates," Latiaris said.

Harpocrates was the Egyptian god of silence. Images show him holding a finger to his lips.

"Can you guarantee that it is true?" Terentius asked.

"The Consul told it to me, but he told me to keep it secret," Pomponius said.

"Lord Latiaris, what's the news?" Minutius asked.

Latiaris said, "I'll tell you, but you must swear to keep it secret —"

He was interrupted by the arrival of Sejanus.

Sejanus said, "I knew the Fates had on their distaff left more of our thread, than so."

The Fates spun the thread of life of each man. Sejanus had been afraid that his life would be cut short, but now he was reassured that he would live long and prosper.

The then-current proverb "to have more tow [flax] on one's distaff than one can spin" means "to have trouble waiting for one."

"Hail, great Sejanus!" Regulus said.

"Hail, the most honored!" Trio the Consul said.

"Happy Sejanus!" Cotta said.

"High Sejanus!" Latiaris said.

"Do you bring prodigies, too?" Sejanus asked.

A prodigy is 1) an omen, or 2) a monster, or 3) a marvel.

Trio said, "May all omens turn to those fair effects, whereof we bring our Lordship news!"

"May it please my lord to withdraw?" Regulus asked.

Sejanus replied, "Yes."

He then said to some people who were standing nearby, "I will speak with you soon."

"My lord, what is your pleasure for the Tribunes?" Terentius asked.

"Why, let them be thanked, and sent away," Sejanus said.

The Tribunes were his bodyguards, whom Sejanus did not think he needed now.

Minutius, Sejanus' friend, began to object, "My lord —"

Laco interrupted, "Will it please Your Lordship to command me?"

"No," Sejanus said. "You're troublesome."

"The mood has changed," Minutius said.

Earlier, Sejanus had been respectful to other people, including Laco.

"Not speak?" the First Tribune asked.

"Nor look?" the Second Tribune asked.

Laco said:

"Aye. He is 'wise' and will make him friends

"Of such who never love but for their ends."

Sejanus would be friends only with people who thought he could help them in some way.

Arruntius and Lepidus stood together.

Some other Senators, including Sanquinius and Haterius, passed by them on their way to see Sejanus.

Arruntius made a commentary on the Senators, who did not overhear him:

"Aye, go, make haste. Take heed that you are not the last person to tender your 'All hail!' in the wide hall of huge Sejanus."

"All hail" was a greeting. The wide hall was where Sejanus met his clients.

Arruntius continued:

"Run a Lictor's pace."

Lictors were quick-footed. They cleared the way for magistrates and made arrests.

Arruntius continued:

"Don't wait to put your robes on, but go, with the pale troubled ensigns — signs — of great friendship stamped in your face!"

Arruntius said:

"Now, Marcus Lepidus, you still believe your former augury?

"Sejanus must go downward? You perceive his wane approaching fast?"

Sejanus seemed to be approaching the highest mark of his life.

"Believe me, Lucius," Lepidus said. "I wonder at this rising of Sejanus!"

Lucius Arruntius replied:

"Aye, and that we must give our vote to it? You will say that it is to make his fall steeper and more grievous?

"It may be so. But those who think that way try with idle wishes to bring back time.

"In desperate cases, all hope is crime.

"See, see! What troops of his officious friends flock to salute my lord! And they appear before my great proud lord, to get a lord-like nod!

"See what they do:

"Attend my lord as he goes to the Senate house!

"Bring back my lord!

"Like servile ushers, make way for my lord!

"Proclaim his idol Lordship, more than ten criers, or a band of six trumpets!

"Bend legs and make bows, kiss hands, and brush a scattered hair from my lord's eminent shoulder!

"See Sanquinius, with his big belly that slows him, and his dropsy! Look what toiling haste he makes! Yet here's another, retarded with and slowed by the gout, who will crowd in front of Sanquinius!

"Get thee Liburnian porters, thou gross fool, to bear thy obsequious fatness, like thy peers.

"They're met! The gout returns, and his great carriage."

He was referring to the gout-ridden Haterius and the overweight Sanquinius.

Some Lictors, the two Consuls, and Sejanus passed by them.

A Lictor called, "Give way! Make place! Room for the Consul!"

"Hail, hail, great Sejanus!" Sanquinius said.

"Hail, my honored lord!" Haterius said.

Everyone except Arruntius and Lepidus exited.

"We shall be noticed and marked soon for our not-hail to Sejanus," Arruntius said.

"That has already been done," Lepidus said.

"It is a note of upstart greatness to observe and watch for these poor trifles, which the noble mind neglects and scorns," Arruntius said.

The poor trifles were the hails to Sejanus.

Lepidus said, "Aye, and they think themselves deeply dishonored where they are omitted, as if they were necessities that helped to the perfection of their dignities and hate the men who just withhold them from them."

Arruntius replied, "Oh, there is a farther cause of hate. Their breasts are guilty that we know their obscure origins and base beginnings. Thence the anger grows. Let's go on and follow them!"

They exited.

Macro and Laco talked together.

Marco said, "When all have entered, shut the temple doors, and bring your guards up to the gate."

"I will," Laco said.

"If you hear commotion in the Senate, present yourself — and charge on any man who attempts to come forth."

"I understand my instructions," Laco said.

They exited.

— 5.10 —

The Senate assembled in the temple of Apollo Palatine.

Present were Heralds, Lictors, Regulus, Sejanus, Trio, Haterius, Sanquinius, Cotta, Pomponius, Latiaris, Lepidus, and Arruntius, along with Natta, a Praetor, and other Senators.

"How well His Lordship looks today!" Haterius said.

"As if he had been born or made for this hour's state," Trio said.

"This hour's state" was "this hour's greatness": The rumor was that Sejanus would be invested with tribunicial power.

"Your fellow Consul's come about, I think?" Cotta said.

The fellow Consul was Regulus, who had been an enemy to Sejanus. Cotta meant that Regulus had come about and was now on the side of Sejanus.

"Aye, he's wise," Trio said.

"Sejanus trusts him well," Sanquinius said.

"Sejanus is a noble, bounteous lord," Trio said.

"He is, indeed, and he is most valiant," Haterius said.

"And most wise," Latiaris said.

"He's everything," the First Senator said.

"He's worthy of all, and more than bounty can bestow," Latiaris said.

"This dignity will make him worthy," Trio said.

"Above Caesar," Pomponius said.

"Tut, Caesar is only the rector — ruler — of an isle," Sanquinius said. "Sejanus is the ruler of the Empire."

"Now he will have power more to reward than ever," Trio said.

Sejanus would have more power than ever to reward those who were loyal to him.

"Let us make sure that we will not be slack in giving him our votes," Cotta said.

"I won't be slack, " Latiaris said.

"Nor I," Sanquinius said.

"The readier we seem to propagate his honors and make them grow, the more we will bind his thought to ours," Cotta said.

They wanted to keep what honors they had — and get more — by being followers of Sejanus.

"I think right with Your Lordship," Haterius said. "It is the way to have us hold our places."

"Aye, and get more," Sanquinius said.

"More official positions, and more titles," Latiaris said.

"I would not lose the part I hope to share in these fortunes of his, for my inheritance," Pomponius said.

"See how Arruntius sits, and Lepidus," Latiaris said.

Other Senators, but not Arruntius and Lepidus, were sitting as close as possible to Sejanus.

Arruntius and Lepidus were definitely not followers of Sejanus.

"Let them alone," Trio said. "They will be marked soon."

"I'll do the same as the others," the First Senator said.

"So will I," the Second Senator said.

"And I," the Third Senator said. "Men grow not in the state except as they are planted warm in his favors."

"Noble Sejanus!" Cotta said loudly so that Sejanus would hear him.

"Honored Sejanus!" Haterius said loudly.

"Worthy and great Sejanus!" Latiaris said loudly.

Noticing this, Arruntius said quietly to Lepidus:

"Gods! How the sponges open and take in! And shut again!

"Look, look!

"Isn't he blest who gets a seat within eye-reach of Sejanus?

"Isn't he more blessed who comes within ear- or tongue-reach?

"Oh, but most blest of all is he who can claw his crafty, cunning elbow, or with a buzz flyblow Sejanus' ears!"

The Praetor said to the Heralds, "Proclaim the Senate's silence, and read out loud the final summons by the edict."

The First Herald shouted, "Silence! In the name of Caesar and the Senate, silence!"

The First Herald then read out loud the final summons:

"Memmius Regulus and Fulcinius Trio, Consuls, these present kalends of June with the first light, shall hold a Senate in the temple of Apollo Palatine."

The kalends of June is June 1, and the year was 31 C.E., but Ben Jonson has the wrong date: Sejanus was actually condemned on 18 October 31 C.E.

The First Herald then continued to read out loud the final summons:

"All who are fathers and are registered fathers who have the right of entering the Senate, we tell you to be in full number present.

"Take knowledge that the business is the commonwealth's.

"Whosoever is absent, his fine or mulct will be taken. His excuse will not be taken."

"Note who are absent, and record their names," Trio ordered.

Regulus the Consul said:

"Fathers conscript, may what I am to utter turn good and happy for the commonwealth.

"And thou, Apollo, god of light and truth, in whose holy house we here are met, inspire us all with truth and with liberty of judgment to our thought.

"The majesty of great Tiberius Caesar propounds to this grave Senate the bestowing upon the man he loves, honored Sejanus, the tribunicial power.

"Here are his letters, signed with his signet.

"What please now the fathers to be done?"

The Senators said, "Read, read them, openly and publicly, read them."

"Caesar has honored his own greatness much in thinking of this act," Cotta said loudly.

"It was a happy thought, and worthy of Caesar," Trio said loudly.

"And the lord as worthy it, on whom it is directed!" Latiaris said loudly.

"Most worthy!" Haterius said loudly.

Sanquinius said loudly, "Rome did never boast the virtue that could give envy bounds, but his: the virtue of Sejanus —"

"Honored and noble!" the First Senator said loudly.

"Good and great Sejanus!" the Second Senator said loudly.

Arruntius said to himself, "Oh, most tame slavery, and ardent flattery!"

The First Herald ordered, "Silence!"

The First Herald then read Tiberius Caesar's epistle — letter — out loud:

"Tiberius Caesar to the Senate, greeting.

"If you conscript fathers, with your children, are in health, it is abundantly well. We with our friends here are so.

"The care of the commonwealth, howsoever we are removed in person, cannot be absent to our thought, although, often, even to princes most present, the truth of their own affairs is hidden, than which nothing falls out more miserable to a state, or makes the art of governing more difficult.

"But since it has been our easeful happiness to enjoy both the aids and industry of so vigilant a Senate, we profess to have been the more indulgent to our pleasures, not as being careless of our office, but rather secure of the necessity."

Tiberius meant that he felt confident that he did not need to be present in Rome because the Senate was capable of handling things in his absence.

The First Herald continued to read Tiberius Caesar's epistle out loud:

"Neither do these common rumors of many and infamous libels published against our retirement at all afflict us, being born more out of men's ignorance than their malice; and will, neglected, find their own grave quickly, whereas too feelingly acknowledged and reacted to, it would make their obloquy ours.

"Nor do we desire that their authors, though found, be censured, since in a free state (as ours) all men ought to enjoy both their minds and tongues free."

Arruntius said to himself, "The lapwing! The lapwing!"

Lapwings are birds that nest on the ground, and they are loudest when away from their nest to keep enemies away from their nestlings. Sometimes they pretend to have an injured wing and cry while leading enemies away from the nest. When the enemy is a safe distance from the nest, the lapwing takes flight. A group of lapwings is called a deceit of lapwings.

The First Herald continued to read Tiberius Caesar's epistle out loud:

"Yet, in things which shall worthily and more nearly concern the majesty of a prince, we shall fear to be so unnaturally cruel to our own fame and reputation as to neglect them.

"True it is, conscript fathers, that we have raised Sejanus from obscure and almost unknown gentry and birth —"

"Hear! Hear!" the Senators said.

The expression means to pay attention to the speaker and implies approval of what is being said.

The First Herald continued to read Tiberius Caesar's epistle out loud:

"— to the highest and most conspicuous point of greatness, and, we hope, deservingly; yet not without danger — it being a most bold hazard in that

sovereign who, by his personal love to one, dares risk the hatred of all his other subjects."

Arruntius said to himself, "This touches; this wounds; the mood changes."

The First Herald continued to read Tiberius Caesar's epistle out loud:

"*But we have faith in your loves and understandings, and do in no way suspect the merit of our Sejanus to make our favors offensive to any —*"

"Oh! Good, good!" the Senators said.

The First Herald continued to read Tiberius Caesar's epistle out loud:

"*— though we could have wished his zeal had run a calmer course against Agrippina and our nephews, howsoever the openness of their actions declared them delinquents; and that he would have remembered no innocence is so safe, but it rejoices to stand in the sight of mercy — the use of which in us he has so completely taken away toward them by his loyal fury, as now our clemency would be thought but wearied cruelty, if we should offer to exercise it.*"

Tiberius Caesar was now openly criticizing Sejanus.

He was obliquely saying that there would be no clemency — mercy — for Sejanus.

Is weariness of cruelty mercy? No.

What is weariness of cruelty? Being so tired of committing cruelty that one stops being cruel. E.g., whipping someone until one's arm grows so tired that one cannot whip that someone any more.

Recognizing what was happening, Arruntius said to himself, "I thank him; there I looked for it. A good fox!"

A proverb of the time stated, "A fox may grow grey but never good."

The First Herald continued to read Tiberius Caesar's epistle out loud:

"*Some there are who would interpret Sejanus' public severity to be personal ambition, and that under a pretext of service to us he does but remove his own hindrances; citing the strengths he has made to himself by the Praetorian soldiers, by his faction in court and Senate, by the offices he holds himself and confers on others, his practice of courting popularity and dependents, his urging (and almost driving) us to this our unwilling retirement, and lastly, his aspiring to be our son-in-law.*"

"This is strange!" the Senators said.

Arruntius said quietly to himself about Marcus Lepidus, "I shall soon believe your vultures, Marcus."

Vultures are birds of omen. Lepidus had speculated about a coming downfall for Sejanus.

The First Herald continued to read Tiberius Caesar's epistle out loud:

"*Your wisdoms, conscript fathers, are able to examine and judge these suggestions. But, were they left to our acquitting verdict, we dare to pronounce them, as we think them, most malicious.*"

"Oh, he has restored all!" the Senators said. "Listen!"

It sounded as if Tiberius were still on the side of Sejanus.

The First Herald continued to read Tiberius Caesar's epistle out loud:

"*Yet are they offered to be averred and proven true, and on the lives of the informers.*

"*What we should say, or rather what we should not say, lords of the Senate, if this should be true, our gods and goddesses confound us if we know!*

"*Only, we must think we have placed our benefits ill; and conclude that in our choice, either we were lacking to the gods, or the gods to us.*"

Now it definitely sounded as if Tiberius were NOT on the side of Sejanus.

The Senators shifted uneasily in their places.

Arruntius said to himself, "The place grows hot; they shift."

The First Herald continued to read Tiberius Caesar's epistle out loud:

"*We have not been desirous, honorable fathers, to change; neither is it now any new lust that alters our affection, or old loathing, but those needful concerns of state, which warn wiser princes, hourly, to provide for their safety, and teach them how learned — deeply read in history — a thing it is to beware of the humblest enemy, much more of those great ones whom their own employed favors have made fit for their fears.*"

"Let's leave!" the First Senator said.

"Let's sit farther away," the Second Senator said.

"Let's remove ourselves," Cotta said.

They suddenly wanted to move away from Sejanus.

Arruntius said to himself, "Gods! How the leaves drop off, even in this little wind!"

The First Herald continued to read Tiberius Caesar's epistle out loud:

"*We therefore desire that the offices he holds be first seized by the Senate and himself suspended from all exercise of place or power —*"

"What!" the Senators said.

Getting up to leave his place near Sejanus, Sanquinius said, "By your leave."

Arruntius said quietly to himself about Sanquinius, "Come, porpoise."

A proverb stated, "The porpoise plays before a storm." In other words, the activity — dancing — of a porpoise was thought to foretell a storm.

"Where's Haterius?" Arruntius asked. "His gout keeps him most miserably constant — in one place."

That place was near Sejanus.

Speaking of Sanquinius, Arruntius said, "Your dancing shows a tempest."

"Read no more," Sejanus said to the First Herald.

"Lords of the Senate, keep your seats," Regulus the Consul said.

He then ordered the First Herald, "Read on."

"These letters, they are forged," Sejanus said.

Regulus called, "A guard!"

Then he ordered everyone, "Sit still."

Laco entered with the guards.

Arruntius said to himself, "Here's change!"

Regulus the Consul said to the First Herald, "Bid the others to be silent, and read forward. Continue to read the epistle out loud."

The First Herald shouted, "Silence!"

The First Herald then continued to read Tiberius Caesar's epistle out loud:

"*— and himself suspended from all exercise of place or power, but until due and mature trial be made of his innocency, which yet we can faintly apprehend the necessity to doubt.*"

One meaning of the word "doubt" at this time is "fear."

The First Herald continued to read Tiberius Caesar's epistle out loud:

"*If, conscript fathers, to your more searching wisdoms there shall appear farther cause — or of farther proceeding, either to seizure of lands, goods, or more — it is not our power that shall limit your authority, or our favor that must corrupt your justice. Either would be dishonorable in you, and both would be uncharitable to ourself.*

"*We would willingly be present with your counsels in this business, but the danger of so potent a faction, if it should prove so, forbids our attempting it, unless one of the Consuls would be entreated for our safety to undertake the guard of us as we return home; then we should most readily risk the journey back to Rome.*

"In the meantime, it shall not be fitting for us to importune and urge so judicious a Senate, who know how much they hurt the innocent by sparing the guilty, and how grateful a sacrifice to the gods is the life of an ingrateful and ungrateful person.

"We reflect not in this on Sejanus — notwithstanding, if you keep an eye upon him — and there is Latiaris, who is a Senator, and Pinnarius Natta, who are two of Sejanus' most trusted ministers, and so professed, whom we desire not to have apprehended, except as the necessity of the cause exacts it."

Regulus the Consul said to a guard, "Put a guard on Latiaris!"

"Oh, the spy!" Arruntius said. "The reverend spy is caught! Who pities him?"

Latiaris was a Senator, and therefore he was reverend.

Arruntius said to Latiaris, "Reward, sir, for your service. Now that you have done your property — your function — you see what use is made of you? And you see how you are treated?"

Under guard, Latiaris and Natta exited.

Arruntius said, "Hang up the instrument."

An instrument is a tool; it can be a person who is made use of.

The image here is of a musical instrument that has been played and is then being hung on a wall.

Attempting to leave, Sejanus said, "Give me leave."

Brandishing his weapon, Laco said, "Stand, stand! He comes upon his death who does advance an inch toward my point."

"Have we no friend here?" Sejanus asked.

"Hushed," Arruntius said. "Where are now all the hails and acclamations?"

Macro entered the scene.

He said, "Hail to the Consuls and to this noble Senate!"

Sejanus said to himself, "Is Macro here? Oh, thou are lost, Sejanus."

The Senators began to rise.

Macro said to the Senators:

"Sit still, and unfrightened, reverend fathers.

"Macro, by Caesar's grace the new-made Provost [Commander of the Praetorian Guard], and now in charge of the Praetorian bands — an honor that recently belonged to that proud man —"

He pointed to Sejanus.

Macro continued, "— bids you to be safe; and to your constant doom — your loyal and firm judgment — of his deservings, offers you the surety — the safety — of all the soldiers, Tribunes, and Centurions received in our command. They will guard and keep you safe."

Regulus the Consul said, "Sejanus! Sejanus!"

Sejanus appeared not to hear.

Regulus called, "Stand forth, Sejanus!"

"Am I called?" Sejanus asked.

Macro said, "Aye, thou, thou insolent monster, are ordered to stand."

Macro used the word "thou" to refer to Sejanus, a word that he would use to speak to an inferior.

Sejanus replied, more courteously than Macro had spoken to him, "Why, Macro, it has been otherwise between you and me! This court, who knows us both, has seen a difference, and can, if it is pleased to speak, confirm whose insolence is most."

Macro said:

"Come down, Typhoeus."

Typhoeus, who had 100 snake heads on his shoulders, was a Titan who attempted but failed to overthrow Jupiter, the King of the gods.

Macro continued:

"If my insolence be most, lo, thus I make it more:

"I kick up thy heels in air, tear off thy robe, and play with thy beard and nostrils."

As Macro mentioned all these actions, he performed them.

Macro continued:

"Thus it is fitting — and let no man take compassion on thy state — let them treat the ingrateful and ungrateful viper as deserved and tread his brains into the earth.

Regulus the Consul said, "Forbear from acting that way. Stop."

Macro replied:

"If I could lose all my humanity now, it would be well to torture so deserving a traitor."

He meant that if he lost all his humanity, he could torture Sejanus as harshly as Sejanus deserved.

Macro continued:

"Wherefore, fathers, do you sit amazed and silent, and do not censure this wretch, who in the hour he first rebelled against Caesar's bounty, did condemn himself?

"Phlegra, the field where all the sons of earth mustered against the gods, never acknowledged so proud and huge a monster."

Phlegra is the battlefield where Jupiter defeated the Titans, aka the sons of earth.

Regulus the Consul ordered, "Take Sejanus away from here. And may all the gods guard Caesar!"

Trio the Consul said to the Lictors, "Take him away from here."

"Hence!" Haterius said.

"To the dungeon with him!" Cotta said.

"He deserves it," Sanquinius said.

"Crown all our doors with laurel wreaths!" the First Senator said.

Laurel wreaths were a sign of victory.

"And let an ox with gilded horns and garlands immediately be led to the Capitol!" Sanquinius said.

"And sacrificed to Jove for Caesar's safety!" Haterius said.

"May all our gods be present still to Caesar!" Trio said.

"Phoebus Apollo!" Cotta said.

"Mars!" Sanquinius said.

"Diana!" Haterius said.

"Pallas Athena!" Sanquinius said.

"Juno, Mercury, all guard him!" the Second Senator said.

Macro said to Sejanus, "Go forth, thou prodigy — monster — of men!"

Under guard, Sejanus exited.

"Let all the traitor's titles be defaced," Cotta said.

"Let his images and statues be pulled down," Trio the Consul said.

"Let his chariot wheels be broken," Haterius said.

Arruntius said sardonically, "And the legs of the poor horses, which have deserved no punishment, let them be broken, too."

They were talking about the chariot wheels and the legs of the horses that were part of the statues of Sejanus.

"O violent change and whirl of men's affections!" Lepidus said.

Arruntius said, "It is as if both their bulks — bodies — and souls were bound on Fortune's wheel and must act only with her motion."

When the wheel of Lady Fortune raises Sejanus high, people treat him one way.

When the wheel of Lady Fortune lowers Sejanus, people treat him a different way.

Macro, Regulus, Trio, Haterius, Sanquinius, etc., exited.

Lepidus, Arruntius, and a few Senators remained behind.

Lepidus said:

"Who would depend upon the shifting popular air and favor, or voice of men, who have today beheld that which, even if all the gods had foredeclared it, would not have been believed: Sejanus' fall?

"He who this morning rose as proudly as the sun, and, breaking through a mist of clients' breath, came on as gazed at and admired as he — the sun — when superstitious Moors salute his light!

"He who had our servile nobles waiting upon him as common servants, and hanging on his look, no less than human life hangs on destiny!

"He who had men's knees bow to him as frequently as they bow to the gods, and who had more sacrifices than Rome had altars —

"And yet this man fall!

"Fall? Aye, without a look who dared to appear his friend, or lend so much of vain relief to his changed state as pity!"

Arruntius said:

"They who before, like gnats, played in his beams, and thronged to encircle him, now not seen! Nor deign to share a bench with him!

"Others, who waited on him and escorted him as he went to the Senate, now inhumanely seize and carry him off to the prison!

"Him whom, just this morning, they followed as their lord, now they guard through the streets, bound like a captured runaway slave!

"Instead of wreaths, they give him fetters; they give him strokes instead of stoops and bows; they give him blind shame instead of honors; and they give him black taunts instead of titles!

"Who would trust slippery chance?"

Lepidus said:

"They who would make themselves her plunder, and foolishly forget that when Lady Fortune flatters, she then comes to prey.

"Lady Fortune, thou would have no deity if men had wisdom. We have placed thee so high because of our foolish belief in thy felicity."

The Senators shouted outside, "The gods guard Caesar! All the gods guard Caesar!"

Macro, Regulus the Consul, and some Senators entered the scene.

Macro said:

"Now, great Sejanus, you who awed the state and sought to bring the nobles to your whip.

"You who would be Caesar's tutor and dispose of dignities and offices; you who had the public always deferential — as shown by their heads being uncovered and bare of hat — to your designs and plots; and you who made the general voice to echo yours, who looked for salutations twelve score off — 240 paces — and would have pyramidal monuments, yea, temples reared to your huge greatness!"

What were called pyramids in this society were often obelisks.

The distance of 240 paces was that of a typical shot of an arrow.

Macro concluded:

"Now you lie as flat as was your pride advanced."

"Thanks to the gods!" Regulus the Consul said.

The Senators said, "And praise to Macro, who has saved Rome! Liberty, liberty, liberty! Lead on! And praise to Macro, who has saved Rome!"

Macro, Regulus, and the Senators exited.

Arruntius and Lepidus remained behind, alone.

Arruntius said, "I prophesy, due to this Senate's flattery, that this new fellow, Macro, will become a greater prodigy — monster — in Rome than he who now has fallen."

Terentius entered the scene and said:

"O you whose minds are good, and have not forced all mankind — all human feeling — from your breasts, who yet have so much stock of virtue left to pity guilty highly-ranked people, when they are wretched:

"Lend your soft, compassionate ears to hear and eyes to weep deeds done by men beyond the acts of Furies.

"The eager multitude, who never yet knew why to love or hate, but only pleased to express their rage of power, no sooner heard the murmuring rumor of Sejanus in decline but, with that speed and heat of appetite with which they greedily run and devour the way to some great sports event or a new theatre —

"They — the eager multitude — filled the Capitol and Pompey's Cirque — his Theater; where, like so many mastiffs, biting stones, as if his statues now were grown sensitive to their wild fury, first they tore the statues down; then fastening ropes to them, they dragged them along the streets, crying in scorn, 'This, this was that rich head that was crowned with garlands and with odors — the smoke of incense — this head that was in Rome so reverenced!

"Now that the furnace and the bellows shall go to work, the great Sejanus shall crack and piece by piece shall drop in the founder's pit."

They were melting the metal of Sejanus' statues so it could be recast as different objects in the founder's pit, which held the molds.

"O popular rage!" Lepidus said.

Terentius said:

"All this while, the Senators, at the temple of Concord, make haste to meet again, and thronging they cry:

"'Let us condemn him, tread him down in water, while he lies upon the bank of the Tiber River. Away!'"

Terentius continued:

"Where some, more tardy, cry unto their bearers — the people carrying them:

"'He will be judged and censured before we come. Run, knaves!'

"And they use that furious diligence, for fear their bondmen should inform against their slackness, and bring their quaking flesh to the hook.

"The rout of men follow with confused voices, crying that they're glad, and they say they could never abide him.

"They inquire: What man was he? What kind of face? What beard did he have? What nose? What lips? They protest that they always did presage he'd come to this.

"They never thought him wise or valiant; they ask after his garments; they ask when he dies? What kind of death?

"And not a beast of all the herd demands: What was his crime? Or, who were his accusers? Under what proof or testimony he fell?

"'There came,' says one, 'a huge, long, worded letter from Capri against him.'

"'Did there so? Oh!'

"They are satisfied with no more evidence than that."

"Alas!" Lepidus said. "They follow Fortune, and hate men who are condemned, whether they are guilty or not."

Arruntius said, "But had Sejanus thrived in his plot, and successfully oppressed the old Tiberius, then, in that same minute, these same rascals in the rabble, who now rage like Furies, would have proclaimed Sejanus Emperor."

"But what has followed these events?" Lepidus asked.

Terentius said:

"He was sentenced by the Senate to lose his head — which was no sooner off, but that head and Sejanus' unfortunate trunk were seized by the rude and ignorant multitude. They, not content with what the eager justice of the state officiously had done, with violent rage have rent his corpse limb from limb.

"A thousand heads, a thousand hands, ten thousand tongues and voices, were employed at once in several different acts of malice!

"Old men were not staid by age, virgins were not staid by shame, recent wives (new widows) were not staid by loss of husbands, mothers were not staid by loss of children."

The word "staid" meant 1) "made sober," and 2) "stayed," aka "held back."

Terentius continued:

"All of them losing all grief in joy of his sad fall, ran quite transported with their cruelty:

"These mounting and jumping at his head and pulling it off the end of a spear, and then these attacking his face, these digging out his eyes, and those with parts of his brain sprinkling themselves, their houses, and their friends.

"Others are met who have ravished thence an arm and deal small pieces of the flesh for favors. These men with a thigh; this man has cut off his hands. And this man has cut off his feet, these men have cut off his fingers, and these men have cut off his toes. That one has his liver; this one has his heart.

"There lacks nothing but room for wrath and place for hatred. Both wrath and hatred are overfilling room and place.

"What cannot often be done is now overdone.

"The whole, and all of what was great Sejanus, and next to Caesar did possess the world, is now torn and scattered, as if he needs no grave.

"Each little part of him is covered by a small amount of dirt and dust.

"So he lies nowhere, and yet he is often buried.

A messenger entered the scene.

"Do you have more information about Sejanus?" Arruntius asked.

"Yes," the messenger said.

"What can be added?" Lepidus asked. "We know that he is dead."

The messenger replied:

"Then there begin your pity.

"There is enough still to come to melt even Rome and Caesar into tears — since never slave could yet so highly offend, but tyranny, in torturing him, would make him worth lamenting.

"A son and daughter to the dead Sejanus, of whom there is not now so much remaining as could be fastened to the hangman's hook, have they drawn forth for farther sacrifice.

"The children's tenderness of knowledge, unripe years, and childish simple innocence was such as scarcely would give them feeling or knowing the danger they were in.

"The girl so simple, as she often asked, Where would they lead her? For what cause did they drag her? She cried that she would do no more wrong. That she could take warning with beating.

"And because our laws allow no immature virgin to die, the cleverly and strangely — unnaturally — cruel Macro delivered her to be deflowered and spoiled by the rude lust of the licentious hangman, then to be strangled with her harmless brother."

The law stated that no immature virgin should be executed. The emphasis was on maturity versus immaturity rather than virginity versus lack of virginity. Sejanus' daughter was immature and suggested that she be spanked as a punishment. Instead, she was given to the executioner, who raped her and then strangled her and her brother.

Lepidus said, "Oh, act most worthy hell and lasting night, so they can hide it from the world!"

The messenger continued:

"Their bodies were thrown onto the Gemonian stairs.

"I don't know how or by what accident she returned to Rome, but the children's mother, the divorced Apicata, found them there.

"When she saw them lying spread on the steps, she unleased a world of fury on herself, tearing her hair, defacing her face, beating her breasts and womb, kneeling distraught, crying to heaven, and then crying to her children.

"At last her drowned voice got up above her woes, and despite her grief, she was able to speak, and with such black and bitter execrations as might frighten the gods and force the sun to run backward to the east — nay, make the old deformed Chaos rise again, to overwhelm them, us, and all the world — she fills the air, upbraids the heavens with their unfair dooms, defies their tyrannous powers, and demands to know what she and those poor innocents have transgressed with the result that they must suffer such a share in vengeance, while Livia, Lygdus, and Eudemus live, who, as she says, and firmly vows to prove it to Caesar and the Senate, poisoned Drusus Senior!"

"Were they confederates with her husband?" Lepidus asked.

"Aye," the messenger answered.

"Strange and unnatural act!" Lepidus said.

"And strangely revealed," Arruntius said. "What says now my monster, the multitude? They reel now after being intoxicated with anger, don't they?"

"Their gall is gone, and now they begin to weep for the evil they have done," the messenger answered.

"I thank them for weeping, the rogues!" Arruntius said.

The messenger said:

"Part are so stupid, or so flexible and easily persuaded, that they believe Sejanus to be innocent. All grieve, and some, whose hands yet reek with his warm blood, and grip the part that they did tear off him, wish that he could be collected and created new."

Lepidus said, "How Fortune plies her sports, when she begins to practice them! Pursues, continues, adds! Confounds and ruins, with varying her impassioned moods!"

Arruntius said:

"Do thou hope, Lady Fortune, to redeem thy crimes? To make amends for thy ill-placed favors with these strange punishments? Forbear, you things that stand upon the pinnacles of state, to boast your slippery height.

"When you do fall, you smash yourselves in pieces, never to rise.

"And he who lends you pity is not wise."

Terentius said:

"Let this example move the insolent man not to grow proud and careless of the gods. It is an odious wisdom — exercise of intelligence — to blaspheme, much more to slighten or deny their powers.

"For whom the morning saw so great and high,

"Thus low and little, before the evening, does lie."

— NOTES —

This tragedy was first acted in the year 1603 by the King's Majesty's Servants.
The principal tragedians were:
RICHARD BURBAGE [Sejanus]
WILLIAM SHAKESPEARE [Probably Tiberius]
AUGUSTINE PHILLIPS
JOHN HEMMINGES
WILLIAM SLY
HENRY CONDELL
JOHN LOWIN
ALEXANDER COOKE
With the allowance of the Master of Revels.

— 1.1 —

[...] I think day
  Should lose its light when men do lose their shames
  And for the empty circumstance — trivial details — of life (200)
  Betray their cause of living.
(Act 1, lines 198-201).
Source of Above:
The Cambridge Edition of the Works of Ben Jonson
7 Volume Set. Volume 2.
Ben Jonson (Author), David Bevington (Editor), Martin Butler (Editor), Ian Donaldson (Editor).
Cambridge University Press, 2012. Print. P. 247.
Juvenal in his eighth Satire, wrote, in G.G. Ramsay's translation:

"[...] count it the greatest of all sins to prefer life to honour, and to lose, for the sake of living, all that makes life worth having." (Juvenal, *Satires* 8.83-84)

Source of Above: G.G. Ramsay. Juvenal, *Satires* (1918). "Satire 8."
https://www.tertullian.org/fathers/juvenal_satires_08.htm

— 1.1 —

TIBERIUS
(One knelt to him.) We will not endure and tolerate these flatteries.
Let him stand.
(Act 1, lines 374-375)
Source of Above:
The Cambridge Edition of the Works of Ben Jonson
7 Volume Set. Volume 2.
Ben Jonson (Author), David Bevington (Editor), Martin Butler (Editor), Ian Donaldson (Editor).
Cambridge University Press, 2012. Print. P. 255.
Suetonius wrote about Tiberius' aversion to flattery. In Alexander Thomson's translation:

He had such an aversion to flattery, that he would never suffer any senator to approach his litter, as he passed the streets in it, either to pay him a civility, or upon business. And when a man of Consular rank, in begging his pardon for some offence he had given him, attempted to fall at his feet, he started from him in such haste, that he stumbled and fell. If any compliment was paid him, either in conversation or a set speech, he would not scruple to interrupt and reprimand the party, and alter what he had said. Being once called "lord," by some person, he desired that he might no more be affronted in that manner. When another, to excite veneration, called his occupations "sacred," and a third had expressed himself thus: "By your authority I have waited upon the senate," he obliged them to change their phrases; in one of them adopting persuasion, instead of "authority," and in the other, laborious, instead of "sacred."

Source of Above:
Suetonius: *The Lives of the Twelve Caesars; An English Translation, Augmented with the Biographies of Contemporary Statesmen, Orators, Poets, and*

Other Associates. Suetonius. Publishing Editor. J. Eugene Reed. Alexander Thomson. Philadelphia. Gebbie & Co. 1889.
http://www.perseus.tufts.edu/hopper/
text?doc=Perseus%3Atext%3A1999.02.0132%3Alife%3Dtib.%3Achapter%3D27

— 2.2 —

It is not safe the children draw long breath,
    That are provokèd by a parent's death.
(Act 2, lines 198-199)
Source of Above:
The Cambridge Edition of the Works of Ben Jonson
7 Volume Set. Volume 2.
Ben Jonson (Author), David Bevington (Editor), Martin Butler (Editor), Ian Donaldson (Editor).
Cambridge University Press, 2012. Print. P. 276.
Aristotle's *Rhetoric*, Book 1, Chapter 15, section 14, states (quoting from *Cypria*, a lost epic):

Foolish is he who, having killed the father, suffers the children to live.

Source of Above:
Aristotle in 23 Volumes, Vol. 22, translated by J. H. Freese. Aristotle. Cambridge and London. Harvard University Press; William Heinemann Ltd. 1926.
http://www.perseus.tufts.edu/hopper/
text?doc=Perseus%3Atext%3A1999.01.0060%3Abook%3D1%3Achapter%3D15

— 2.2 —

Εμου θανοντος γαια μιχθητω πυρι.
   (Act 2, line 330)
   Source of Above:
   The Cambridge Edition of the Works of Ben Jonson
   7 Volume Set. Volume 2.
   Ben Jonson (Author), David Bevington (Editor), Martin Butler (Editor), Ian Donaldson (Editor).
   Cambridge University Press, 2012. Print. P. 282.
   The Greek means:

   When I am dead, may earth be overwhelmed with fire.

   Source of Above:
   The Greek Anthology, Book 7. 704. Trans. W.R. Paton. Loeb Classical Library.
   https://www.loebclassics.com/view/greek_anthology_7/1917/pb_LCL068.375.xml

— 2.2 —

Thy thoughts are ours, in all, and we but tested (280)
Their voice, in our designs, which by assenting
Hath more confirmed us than if heart'ning Jove
Had, from his hundred statues, bid us strike,
And at the stroke clicked all his marble thumbs.
(Act 2, lines 280-284)
Source of Above:
The Cambridge Edition of the Works of Ben Jonson
7 Volume Set. Volume 2.
Ben Jonson (Author), David Bevington (Editor), Martin Butler (Editor), Ian Donaldson (Editor).
Cambridge University Press, 2012. Print. P. 279-280.
The below information is an excerpt from an article titled "THE TRUTH ABOUT GLADIATORS AND THE THUMBS UP":

> *The fate of a gladiator, in terms of whether the audience was voting for a kill, was decided with what is known as "pollice verso", a Latin term which roughly translates to "turned thumb". More precisely what this means isn't known and there are no accounts that have survived to this day that describe it in any real detail. As such, we're unable to say for sure which way the thumb was supposed to be pointed if the audience wanted a given gladiator to be killed or if they could just wave their thumbs around at random, which it seems may well have been the case.*
>
> *So that's voting for death, what about life? The gesture to spare a given gladiator's life seems to have been neither a thumbs up nor a thumbs down. Instead, you had to hide your thumb inside your fist, forming a gesture known as pollice compresso, "compressed thumb".*

Source: Karl Smallwood. "THE TRUTH ABOUT GLADIATORS AND THE THUMBS UP." Today I Found Out. 23 October 2014. Accessed 17 February 2022

168

http://www.todayifoundout.com/index.php/2014/10/give-thumbs-gesture-get-start/

— 2.3 —

Were all Tiberius' body stuck with eyes, (450)
And every wall and hanging in my house
Transparent as this lawn I wear, or air;
Yea, had Sejanus both his ears as long
As to my inmost closet, I would hate
To whisper any thought, or change an act, (455)
To be made Juno's rival. Virtue's forces
Show ever noblest in conspicuous courses.
(Act 2, lines 450-457)
Source of Above:
The Cambridge Edition of the Works of Ben Jonson
7 Volume Set. Volume 2.
Ben Jonson (Author), David Bevington (Editor), Martin Butler (Editor), Ian Donaldson (Editor).
Cambridge University Press, 2012. Print. P. 287-288.
The below is a quotation from my book *Virgil's* Aeneid: *A Retelling in Prose*:

Rumor has wings and many feathers. Her many eyes never sleep, and she has many tongues and many ears. By night she flies, and by day she watches and listens. She values lies as much as she values truths.

Source of Above: David Bruce, *Virgil's* Aeneid: *A Retelling in Prose*.
https://www.smashwords.com/books/view/277646

— 3.1 —

Augustus well foresaw what we should suffer
*   Under Tiberius, when he did pronounce (485)*
*   The Roman race most wretched that should live*
*   Between so slow jaws, and so long a-bruising.*
(Act 3, lines 484-487)
Source of Above:
The Cambridge Edition of the Works of Ben Jonson
7 Volume Set. Volume 2.
Ben Jonson (Author), David Bevington (Editor), Martin Butler (Editor), Ian Donaldson (Editor).
Cambridge University Press, 2012. Print. P. 312.
Suetonius, in his "Life of Tiberius" (*Lives* III.21), wrote:

I know, it is generally believed, that upon Tiberius's quitting the room, after their private conference, those who were in waiting overheard Augustus say, "Ah! unhappy Roman people, to be ground by the jaws of such a slow devourer!"

Source of Above:
Suetonius: *The Lives of the Twelve Caesars; An English Translation, Augmented with the Biographies of Contemporary Statesmen, Orators, Poets, and Other Associates.* Suetonius. Publishing Editor. J. Eugene Reed. Alexander Thomson [translator]. Philadelphia. Gebbie & Co. 1889.
https://www.perseus.tufts.edu/hopper/
text?doc=Perseus%3Atext%3A1999.02.0132%3Alife%3Dtib.%3Achapter%3D21

<h1 style="text-align:center">— 3.2 —</h1>

I have heard Augustus, (515)
In the bestowing of his daughter, thought
But even of gentlemen of Rome.
(Act 3, Lines 515-517)
Source of Above:
The Cambridge Edition of the Works of Ben Jonson
7 Volume Set. Volume 2.
Ben Jonson (Author), David Bevington (Editor), Martin Butler (Editor), Ian Donaldson (Editor).
Cambridge University Press, 2012. Print. P. 313.

Note by David Bruce: Sejanus was a member of the equestrian class of citizens, which were ranked just below the noble class. Marriages could be arranged between the children of the two classes to strength alliances. Sejanus' daughter had been betrothed to a son of the future emperor Claudius, but a few days later, Claudius' son died, according to Suetonius, by choking to death on a pear he had thrown into the air and caught in his mouth.

See Suetonius, *The Lives of the Twelve Caesars*, "Life of Claudius," 27.

https://www.perseus.tufts.edu/hopper/
text?doc=Perseus%3Atext%3A1999.02.0132%3Alife%3Dcl.%3Achapter%3D27

— 4.1 —

Was Silius safe? Or the good Sosia safe? (20)
Or was my niece, dear Claudia Pulchra, safe?
Or innocent Furnius?
(Act 4, lines 22-22)
Source of Above:
The Cambridge Edition of the Works of Ben Jonson
7 Volume Set. Volume 2.
Ben Jonson (Author), David Bevington (Editor), Martin Butler (Editor), Ian Donaldson (Editor).
Cambridge University Press, 2012. Print. P. 323-324.
The below is Tacitus, *Annals*, Book 4, Chapter 52:

At Rome meanwhile, besides the shocks already sustained by the imperial house, came the first step towards the destruction of Agrippina, Claudia Pulchra, her cousin, being prosecuted by Domitius Afer. Lately a prætor, a man of but moderate position and eager to become notorious by any sort of deed, Afer charged her with unchastity, with having Furnius for her paramour, and with attempts on the emperor by poison and sorcery. Agrippina, always impetuous, and now kindled into fury by the peril of her kinswoman, went straight to Tiberius and found him, as it happened, offering a sacrifice to his father. This provoked an indignant outburst. "It is not," she exclaimed, "for the same man to slay victims to the Divine Augustus and to persecute his posterity. The celestial spirit has not transferred itself to the mute statue; here is the true image, sprung of heavenly blood, and she perceives her danger, and assumes its mournful emblems. Pulchra's name is a mere blind; the only reason for her destruction is that she has, in utter folly, selected Agrippina for her admiration, forgetting that Sosia was thereby ruined." These words wrung from the emperor one of the rare utterances of that inscrutable breast; he rebuked Agrippina with a Greek verse, and reminded her that "she was not wronged because she was not a queen." Pulchra and Furnius were condemned. Afer was ranked with

173

the foremost orators, for the ability which he displayed, and which won strong praise from Tiberius, who pronounced him a speaker of natural genius. Henceforward as a counsel for the defence or the prosecution he enjoyed the fame of eloquence rather than of virtue, but old age robbed him of much of his speaking power, while, with a failing intellect, he was still impatient of silence.

Source of Above:
Tacitus, *Annals*, Book 4, Chapter 52.
Complete Works of Tacitus. Tacitus. Alfred John Church. William Jackson Brodribb. Sara Bryant. edited for Perseus. New York: Random House, Inc. Random House, Inc. reprinted 1942.

http://www.perseus.tufts.edu/hopper/
text?doc=Perseus%3Atext%3A1999.02.0078%3Abook%3D4%3Achapter%3D52

— 4.3 —

Here place yourselves, between the roof and ceiling, (95)
(4.95)
Source of Above:
The Cambridge Edition of the Works of Ben Jonson
7 Volume Set. Volume 2.
Ben Jonson (Author), David Bevington (Editor), Martin Butler (Editor),
Ian Donaldson (Editor).
Cambridge University Press, 2012. Print. P. 327.
The below is Tacitus, *Annals*, Book 4, Chapter 69:

The men whom I have named now consulted how these conversations might fall within the hearing of more persons. It was necessary that the place of meeting should preserve the appearance of secrecy, and, if witnesses were to stand behind the doors, there was a fear of their being seen or heard, or of suspicion casually arising. Three senators thrust themselves into the space between the roof and ceiling, a hiding-place as shameful as the treachery was execrable. They applied their ears to apertures and crevices. Latiaris meanwhile having met Sabinus in the streets, drew him to his house and to the room, as if he was going to communicate some fresh discoveries. There he talked much about past and impending troubles, a copious topic indeed, and about fresh horrors. Sabinus spoke as before and at greater length, as sorrow, when once it has broken into utterance, is the harder to restrain. Instantly they hastened to accuse him, and having despatched a letter to the emperor, they informed him of the order of the plot and of their own infamy. Never was Rome more distracted and terror-stricken. Meetings, conversations, the ear of friend and stranger were alike shunned; even things mute and lifeless, the very roofs and walls, were eyed with suspicion.

Source of Above:
Tacitus, *Annals*, Book 4, Chapter 69.

Complete Works of Tacitus. Tacitus. Alfred John Church. William Jackson Brodribb. Sara Bryant. edited for Perseus. New York: Random House, Inc. Random House, Inc. reprinted 1942.

http://www.perseus.tufts.edu/hopper/

text?doc=Perseus%3Atext%3A1999.02.0078%3Abook%3D4%3Achapter%3D69

The *Annals* (From the Passing of the Divine Augustus) (1876) by Tacitus, translated by Alfred John Church and William Jackson Brodribb.

https://en.wikisource.org/wiki/The_Annals_(Tacitus)

In real life, "the space between the roof and ceiling" would be an attic, but what would that space be on the stage?

I think it would be the upper stage, which is under the roof and whose floor forms a ceiling for part of the lower stage.

— 4.5 —

Some are allured, (395)
> *Some threatened; others, by their friends detained,*
> *Are ravished hence like captives, and, in sight*
> *Of their most grievèd parents, dealt away*
> *Unto his spintries, sellaries, and slaves,*
> *Masters of strange and new-commented lusts, (400)*
> *For which wise nature hath not left a name.*

Source of Above:

The Cambridge Edition of the Works of Ben Jonson

7 Volume Set. Volume 2.

Ben Jonson (Author), David Bevington (Editor), Martin Butler (Editor), Ian Donaldson (Editor).

Cambridge University Press, 2012. Print. P. 341.

According to the *Oxford English Dictionary*, spintries and sellaries are male prostitutes. Suetonius wrote about spintries and sellaries in his *The Lives of the Twelve Caesars*, "Life of Tiberius," section 43, but frequently some of what he wrote is not translated in older books out of modesty. Sometimes the most salacious parts are left in Latin, untranslated, and put in an appendix.

This is section 43 of Suetonius, *Lives*, "Life of Tiberius," uncensored:

> *On retiring to Capri he devised a pleasance for his secret orgies: teams of wantons of both sexes, selected as experts in deviant intercourse and dubbed analists, copulated before him in triple unions to excite his flagging passions. Its bedrooms were furnished with the most salacious paintings and sculptures, as well as with an erotic library, in case a performer should need an illustration of what was required. Then in Capri's woods and groves he arranged a number of nooks of venery where boys and girls got up as Pans and nymphs solicited outside bowers and grottoes: people openly called this "the old goat's garden," punning on the island's name.*

Source of Above:

177

Suetonius *Lives*, "Life of Tiberius." Section 43. Trans. J.C. Rolfe.
https://penelope.uchicago.edu/Thayer/e/roman/texts/suetonius/
12caesars/tiberius*.html
A discussion of the word "spintriae" occurs here:
https://humanities.classics.narkive.com/p88vT0Qg/spintriae
A "sellary" may be defined in this way:

*A large sitting-room, drawing room, or reception room that is furnished
with chairs or benches.*

McGraw-Hill Dictionary of Architecture and Construction. Copyright ©
2003 by McGraw-Hill Companies, Inc.
This definition is not found in the *Oxford English Dictionary*.

APPENDIX A: FAIR USE

This communication uses information that I have downloaded and adapted from the WWW. I will not make a dime from it. The use of this information is consistent with fair use:

§ 107. Limitations on exclusive rights: Fair use

Release date: 2004-04-30

Notwithstanding the provisions of sections 106 and 106A, the fair use of a copyrighted work, including such use by reproduction in copies or phonorecords or by any other means specified by that section, for purposes such as criticism, comment, news reporting, teaching (including multiple copies for classroom use), scholarship, or research, is not an infringement of copyright. In determining whether the use made of a work in any particular case is a fair use the factors to be considered shall include —

(1) the purpose and character of the use, including whether such use is of a commercial nature or is for nonprofit educational purposes;

(2) the nature of the copyrighted work;

(3) the amount and substantiality of the portion used in relation to the copyrighted work as a whole; and

(4) the effect of the use upon the potential market for or value of the copyrighted work.

The fact that a work is unpublished shall not itself bar a finding of fair use if such finding is made upon consideration of all the above factors.

Source of Fair Use information:

<http://www.law.cornell.edu/uscode/17/107.html>

APPENDIX B: ABOUT THE AUTHOR

It was a dark and stormy night. Suddenly a cry rang out, and on a hot summer night in 1954, Josephine, wife of Carl Bruce, gave birth to a boy — me. Unfortunately, this young married couple allowed Reuben Saturday, Josephine's brother, to name their first-born. Reuben, aka "The Joker," decided that Bruce was a nice name, so he decided to name me Bruce Bruce. I have gone by my middle name — David — ever since.

Being named Bruce David Bruce hasn't been all bad. Bank tellers remember me very quickly, so I don't often have to show an ID. It can be fun in charades, also. When I was a counselor as a teenager at Camp Echoing Hills in Warsaw, Ohio, a fellow counselor gave the signs for "sounds like" and "two words," then she pointed to a bruise on her leg twice. Bruise Bruise? Oh yeah, Bruce Bruce is the answer!

Uncle Reuben, by the way, gave me a haircut when I was in kindergarten. He cut my hair short and shaved a small bald spot on the back of my head. My mother wouldn't let me go to school until the bald spot grew out again.

Of all my brothers and sisters (six in all), I am the only transplant to Athens, Ohio. I was born in Newark, Ohio, and have lived all around Southeastern Ohio. However, I moved to Athens to go to Ohio University and have never left.

At Ohio U, I never could make up my mind whether to major in English or Philosophy, so I got a bachelor's degree with a double major in both areas, then I added a Master of Arts degree in English and a Master of Arts degree in Philosophy. Yes, I have my MAMA degree.

Currently, and for a long time to come (I eat fruits and veggies), I am spending my retirement writing books such as *Nadia Comaneci: Perfect 10*, *The Funniest People in Comedy*, *Homer's* Iliad: *A Retelling in Prose*, and *William Shakespeare's* Hamlet: *A Retelling in Prose*.

By the way, my sister Brenda Kennedy writes romances such as *A New Beginning* and *Shattered Dreams*.

APPENDIX C: SOME BOOKS BY DAVID BRUCE

Retellings of a Classic Work of Literature

Arden of Faversham: *A Retelling*

Ben Jonson's The Alchemist: *A Retelling*

Ben Jonson's The Arraignment, or Poetaster: *A Retelling*

Ben Jonson's Bartholomew Fair: *A Retelling*

Ben Jonson's The Case is Altered: *A Retelling*

Ben Jonson's Catiline's Conspiracy: *A Retelling*

Ben Jonson's The Devil is an Ass: *A Retelling*

Ben Jonson's Epicene: *A Retelling*

Ben Jonson's Every Man in His Humor: *A Retelling*

Ben Jonson's Every Man Out of His Humor: *A Retelling*

Ben Jonson's The Fountain of Self-Love, or Cynthia's Revels: *A Retelling*

Ben Jonson's The Magnetic Lady, or Humors Reconciled: *A Retelling*

Ben Jonson's The New Inn, or The Light Heart: *A Retelling*

Ben Jonson's Sejanus' Fall: *A Retelling*

Ben Jonson's The Staple of News: *A Retelling*

Ben Jonson's A Tale of a Tub: *A Retelling*

Ben Jonson's Volpone, or the Fox: *A Retelling*

Christopher Marlowe's Complete Plays: Retellings

Christopher Marlowe's Dido, Queen of Carthage: *A Retelling*

Christopher Marlowe's Doctor Faustus: *Retellings of the 1604 A-Text and of the 1616 B-Text*

Christopher Marlowe's Edward II: *A Retelling*

Christopher Marlowe's The Massacre at Paris: *A Retelling*

Christopher Marlowe's The Rich Jew of Malta: *A Retelling*

Christopher Marlowe's Tamburlaine, Parts 1 and 2: *Retellings*

Dante's Divine Comedy: *A Retelling in Prose*

Dante's Inferno: *A Retelling in Prose*

Dante's Purgatory: *A Retelling in Prose*

Dante's Paradise: *A Retelling in Prose*

The Famous Victories of Henry V: *A Retelling*

From the Iliad *to the* Odyssey: *A Retelling in Prose of Quintus of Smyrna's* Posthomerica

George Chapman, Ben Jonson, and John Marston's Eastward Ho! *A Retelling*

George Peele's The Arraignment of Paris: *A Retelling*

George Peele's The Battle of Alcazar: *A Retelling*

George Peele's David and Bathsheba, and the Tragedy of Absalom: *A Retelling*

George Peele's Edward I: *A Retelling*

George Peele's The Old Wives' Tale: *A Retelling*

George-a-Greene: *A Retelling*

The History of King Leir: *A Retelling*

Homer's Iliad: *A Retelling in Prose*

Homer's Odyssey: *A Retelling in Prose*

J.W. Gent.'s The Valiant Scot: *A Retelling*

Jason and the Argonauts: A Retelling in Prose of Apollonius of Rhodes' Argonautica

John Ford: Eight Plays Translated into Modern English

John Ford's The Broken Heart: *A Retelling*

John Ford's The Fancies, Chaste and Noble: *A Retelling*

John Ford's The Lady's Trial: *A Retelling*

John Ford's The Lover's Melancholy: *A Retelling*

John Ford's Love's Sacrifice: *A Retelling*

John Ford's Perkin Warbeck: *A Retelling*

John Ford's The Queen: *A Retelling*

John Ford's 'Tis Pity She's a Whore: *A Retelling*

John Lyly's Campaspe: *A Retelling*

John Lyly's Endymion, The Man in the Moon: *A Retelling*

John Lyly's Galatea: *A Retelling*

John Lyly's Love's Metamorphosis: *A Retelling*

John Lyly's Midas: *A Retelling*

John Lyly's Mother Bombie: *A Retelling*

John Lyly's Sappho and Phao: *A Retelling*

John Lyly's The Woman in the Moon: *A Retelling*

John Webster's The White Devil: *A Retelling*

King Edward III: *A Retelling*

Mankind: *A Medieval Morality Play* (A Retelling)

Margaret Cavendish's The Unnatural Tragedy: *A Retelling*

The Merry Devil of Edmonton: *A Retelling*

The Summoning of Everyman: *A Medieval Morality Play* (A Retelling)

Robert Greene's Friar Bacon and Friar Bungay: *A Retelling*

The Taming of a Shrew: *A Retelling*

Tarlton's Jests: A Retelling

Thomas Middleton's A Chaste Maid in Cheapside: *A Retelling*

Thomas Middleton's Women Beware Women: *A Retelling*

Thomas Middleton and Thomas Dekker's The Roaring Girl: *A Retelling*

Thomas Middleton and William Rowley's The Changeling: *A Retelling*

The Trojan War and Its Aftermath: Four Ancient Epic Poems

Virgil's Aeneid: *A Retelling in Prose*

William Shakespeare's 5 Late Romances: Retellings in Prose

William Shakespeare's 10 Histories: Retellings in Prose

William Shakespeare's 11 Tragedies: Retellings in Prose

William Shakespeare's 12 Comedies: Retellings in Prose

William Shakespeare's 38 Plays: Retellings in Prose
William Shakespeare's 1 Henry IV, aka Henry IV, Part 1: *A Retelling in Prose*
William Shakespeare's 2 Henry IV, aka Henry IV, Part 2: *A Retelling in Prose*
William Shakespeare's 1 Henry VI, aka Henry VI, Part 1: *A Retelling in Prose*
William Shakespeare's 2 Henry VI, aka Henry VI, Part 2: *A Retelling in Prose*
William Shakespeare's 3 Henry VI, aka Henry VI, Part 3: *A Retelling in Prose*
William Shakespeare's All's Well that Ends Well: *A Retelling in Prose*
William Shakespeare's Antony and Cleopatra: *A Retelling in Prose*
William Shakespeare's As You Like It: *A Retelling in Prose*
William Shakespeare's The Comedy of Errors: *A Retelling in Prose*
William Shakespeare's Coriolanus: *A Retelling in Prose*
William Shakespeare's Cymbeline: *A Retelling in Prose*
William Shakespeare's Hamlet: *A Retelling in Prose*
William Shakespeare's Henry V: *A Retelling in Prose*
William Shakespeare's Henry VIII: *A Retelling in Prose*
William Shakespeare's Julius Caesar: *A Retelling in Prose*
William Shakespeare's King John: *A Retelling in Prose*
William Shakespeare's King Lear: *A Retelling in Prose*
William Shakespeare's Love's Labor's Lost: *A Retelling in Prose*
William Shakespeare's Macbeth: *A Retelling in Prose*
William Shakespeare's Measure for Measure: *A Retelling in Prose*
William Shakespeare's The Merchant of Venice: *A Retelling in Prose*
William Shakespeare's The Merry Wives of Windsor: *A Retelling in Prose*
William Shakespeare's A Midsummer Night's Dream: *A Retelling in Prose*
William Shakespeare's Much Ado About Nothing: *A Retelling in Prose*
William Shakespeare's Othello: *A Retelling in Prose*
William Shakespeare's Pericles, Prince of Tyre: *A Retelling in Prose*
William Shakespeare's Richard II: *A Retelling in Prose*
William Shakespeare's Richard III: *A Retelling in Prose*
William Shakespeare's Romeo and Juliet: *A Retelling in Prose*
William Shakespeare's The Taming of the Shrew: *A Retelling in Prose*
William Shakespeare's The Tempest: *A Retelling in Prose*
William Shakespeare's Timon of Athens: *A Retelling in Prose*
William Shakespeare's Titus Andronicus: *A Retelling in Prose*
William Shakespeare's Troilus and Cressida: *A Retelling in Prose*
William Shakespeare's Twelfth Night: *A Retelling in Prose*
William Shakespeare's The Two Gentlemen of Verona: *A Retelling in Prose*
William Shakespeare's The Two Noble Kinsmen: *A Retelling in Prose*
William Shakespeare's The Winter's Tale: *A Retelling in Prose*